Praise for Asexual Fairy Tales

"Fairy tales are a part of every child's life. As we grow up, we learn mythology, history, and legends. Yet, for asexuals, the representation has always been rare to non-existent. What Elizabeth Hopkinson has done is brought aces to the forefront in these pieces of writing. It's an incredible and necessary thing! Everyone wants to see a character that is like themselves in what they read or watch, even when it comes to fairy tales. So what Elizabeth is doing here is greatly appreciated, and we wish her the very best!"
— Kelsey Lee, Social Media Director of AVEN

'Elizabeth Hopkinson is a natural storyteller and her fairy tales are compelling, powerful and full of the numinous.'
— Dr Teika Bellamy, Mother's Milk Books

"These Asexual Fairy Tales sound like old folk tales, perfect for reading out loud. More than just a retelling or adaptation, Elizabeth has succeeded in creating something new without losing that old-world storyteller feel."
— Jaylee James, editor of *Circuits and Slippers*

ELIZABETH HOPKINSON is the author of over eighty published short stories. Her work has appeared in the likes of *The Forgotten & the Fantastical* and *Dancing with Mr Darcy* anthologies. She is the winner of the James White Award and Fairytalez Best Gender Swap Fairy Tale. Her novel *Silver Hands* is a re-imagining of 'The Handless Maiden' set in the Golden Age of Sail. She is currently working on a trilogy about a castrato and a bird charmer and a stand-alone novel based on 'The Ice Queen and the Mer-King'.

ANNA HOPKINSON is an illustration student at the University of Huddersfield. This is her first publication.

Elizabeth and Anna both live in Bradford, West Yorkshire, in a tiny house that is gradually being taken over by books, artwork and cat toys.

You can visit Elizabeth's website at: elizabethhopkinson.co.uk
To see more of Anna's work visit her instagram: annahopkinson_art

Asexual

Fairy

Tales

Elizabeth Hopkinson

SilverWood

Published in 2019 by SilverWood Books

SilverWood Books Ltd
14 Small Street, Bristol, BS1 1DE, United Kingdom
www.silverwoodbooks.co.uk

ISBN 978-1-78132-894-1 (paperback)
ISBN 978-1-78132-895-8 (ebook)

British Library Cataloguing in Publication Data
A CIP catalogue record for this book is available
from the British Library

Page design and typesetting by SilverWood Books
Printed on responsibly sourced paper

To Mick, for understanding

Contents

From the Author

Fairy tales have always been central to our experience as human beings. They help us deal with difficult, complex and even taboo subjects, turning our inner struggles into fights with dragons or escapes from castles.

But what happens when you belong to an invisible minority? Around one per cent of the population identifies as asexual. (That is, people who do not experience sexual attraction). But most people have never even heard of asexuality. Others deny that it really exists or see it as a problem to be fixed. In contemporary culture, it often seems there is little or no representation of asexuals and our perspectives. Our ancestors, on the other hand, seemed much more honest and open about the spectrum of human sexuality. There are many fairy tales and myths that apparently contain asexual characters or use motifs that speak to asexual issues and struggles.

These are the tales I have gathered together in this book. They come from diverse sources: from *Grimm's Fairy Tales* to the *Thousand and One Nights*, from Greek mythology to the Arthurian legend, from Scandinavia to Japan. Alongside these are my own re-imaginings and original tales based on traditional motifs, most of which were previously published in other anthologies and magazines.

Asexuality covers a broad spectrum, and I'm aware that the tales in this book won't relate to everyone's experience. But these are the stories that helped me. I hope they will help someone else.

I exist and I am proud!

Elizabeth Hopkinson, 2019

The Origin of Love

1

The Origin of Love

'The Origin of Love' comes from *Symposium*, written by the Greek philosopher Plato in 360 BC. *Symposium* takes the form of an imaginary discussion between friends, who are debating the nature of love. It is the origin of our term, Platonic love. This tale is told by one of the companions, Aristophanes. It is an origin tale, explaining why humans are always looking for their "other half". My retelling is based on a translation by Benjamin Jowett on the *Internet Classics Archive*.

Once upon a time, humans were not as they are now. There were not two sexes but three: male, female and a combination of the two. The man was the child of the sun, the woman the child of the earth, and the man-woman the child of the moon.

These humans were round in shape, just like their heavenly parents. Each person had two faces, which looked out in opposite directions, four hands, four feet, and so on. They were joined back-to-back, and the part in-between was round, like an apple. In this shape, they could walk forwards or backwards, or any direction they pleased. And if they wanted to move quickly, they could roll over and over like tumblers, using their hands and feet.

The three kinds of people were happy and contented with their lives. They explored the earth, tamed animals, built villages. When they wanted to have children, they laid eggs in the grass, which they self-fertilised and brooded until they hatched.

In time, humans came to build cities, with great pyramids and aqueducts to water the land. Because of this, the gods feared their power, afraid that humans might try to scale heaven itself. They debated among themselves what they should do about this new threat. Should they annihilate the human race, as they had done with the race of giants? But, if they did so, who then would offer sacrifices to the gods?

At last, Zeus had an idea. "I will cut them in half. That way, they will be less powerful, and there will be more of them to offer sacrifices."

So, Zeus cut the humans in half, so each had only one head, two hands and two feet. He sent Apollo to heal their wounds and mould their shape, so their backs were no longer round. And he threatened that, if humans did not behave, he would cut them again, so each had only one leg on which to hop.

Now they were cut in half, the humans were no longer content, but lonely. Each one went seeking for the other half they had known: men seeking women, women seeking men, men seeking men and women seeking women. Each sought the person that housed the missing part of their soul. If they chanced to find their missing half, the two clung together, longing that they might be melded into one, as they had been previously.

This is the origin of love. It is born from the longing of two souls that desire to be one and is a spiritual impulse. But, when Zeus saw how frustrated humans were that they could not meld back together, he took pity on them. He turned their reproductive organs around to the front, where they had never been before. Those who wished it could join bodily through their organs, for comfort and for the conception of children.

But the highest love was, and always will be, the love of the soul. So said the philosopher Plato, in the story you have just read. And that is why we call this kind of love Platonic.

The Glass Coffin

2

The Glass Coffin

The next two tales are mirror versions of one another, telling a very similar story from first a female and then a male perspective. 'The Glass Coffin' is the feminine version of the tale. It tells of a Tailor seeking his fortune and a Girl imprisoned in glass by a Sorcerer. I have always been drawn to the motif of the glass coffin as a symbol of inviolate femininity. But what I also like about this story is the sexless partnership of Girl, Brother and Tailor overcoming the lecherous advances of the Sorcerer.

'The Glass Coffin' comes from *Grimm's Household Stories* (1853). A much-shortened version can be found under the title 'The Crystal Coffin' in Andrew Lang's *Green Fairy Book* (1892). My version also owes a debt to A S Byatt's masterly retelling in her novel, *Possession* (1990).

There once lived a journeyman Tailor, neither handsome like a prince nor bold like a knight, but slender and somewhat timid. He had become lost in a wood at night and, afraid of wild beasts, had climbed a tree for safety. From his perch on a wide branch, he espied a light among the trees that might just be a candle in a cottage window.

The Tailor clambered down and picked his way along the woodland path by what moonlight was visible, stumbling over roots until he came to the humblest cottage you could imagine, woven from reeds and rushes with a moss roof.

The Tailor knocked at the door. It was opened by an old, old man with a rushlight in his hand, the smoke of which wreathed about his head. His eyes were a piercing green, swirling with depths of yet darker green like the colours of the forest itself.

"What do you want?" The old man's voice rasped like dry leaves.

"P-please," said the Tailor, who was shivering with cold. "May I have a place by your fireside for the night? I have no money to give, but I could repay you by working."

"I know your sort of work." The old man scowled. "To kill and rob an old man while he sleeps." He made as if to shut the door.

Desperation emboldened the Tailor. He stuck his foot in the door.

"No, no, truly. I have no weapon worse than a needle and scissors." He held up the tools of his trade for the old man to see. "I am only an honest Tailor. I'm afraid I have no money to give or food to share, but I could do a little mending in return for your kindness." He glanced at the frayed cuff of the old man's coat.

The old man gave a secret smile.

"Is that so? Well, you'd better come in, Tailor, although I've no need of your services. But I think destiny has led you here tonight."

The Tailor followed the old man into the cottage. By the light of the fire, he could see that the old man's coat was a patchwork of many different kinds of material, and that some were of the oddest sort. One patch was of cobwebs glittering with hoar-frost, another the delicate skeletons of autumn leaves. The old man moved nimbly about the cottage like someone half his age, collecting straw and piles of rags to make the Tailor's bed. Thanking the man, the Tailor stretched out before the fire and was soon fast asleep.

In the morning, the Tailor was sure to stoke up the fire, and to collect fresh water from the stream outside the cottage, so the old man could make breakfast. The man nodded his approval and, when the meal was done, he took off his patchwork coat and gave it to the Tailor.

"As a man who makes garments, you will surely appreciate this gift," he said.

"I couldn't possibly accept this." The Tailor tried to give the coat back. "It's...it's a marvel of stitchery. Besides, you'll need it to warm your bones."

The old man gave a wink.

"You'll need it more, my lad. Trust me."

He took a small cauldron of hot water from its hook above the fire.

"Now, take this," he said, "and cast it upon a large stone slab you will see not far from here. But take my advice. Whatever you see as a result, be sure to ask of it the question: *What is the meaning of this sign?* Then all will go well for you. Others have failed in this quest, but I think

20

this time will be different. Many knights and princes have come this way seeking adventure, but never a tailor."

"I sought nothing but shelter..." the Tailor began, but the old man hushed him and placed the cauldron in his hand.

"The stone slab," he said.

Baffled, the Tailor put the patchwork coat on his back and carried the cauldron of hot water to the stone slab. As the old man had bidden, he cast the water upon the stone.

A great steam arose. Then came a thundering of hooves, and into the clearing came a great Ox with horns of iron. The Tailor began to tremble. He had sought the cottage to escape fearsome beasts, and now one was galloping towards him.

But at the next moment, more hoofbeats came from the opposite direction, and a Stag with a golden collar about its neck charged the Ox. The Stag seemed such a slender creature, the Tailor was sure the Ox would gore it to death. In fact, he could see scars on the Stag's flank that looked like the previous marks of iron horns. The two circled and charged, circled and charged, their horns clashing violently and the ground shaking beneath their hooves. The Tailor was too afraid to move.

Then he remembered the old man's instructions. He cleared his dry throat and spoke the words:

"What is the meaning of this sign?"

As soon as the words were spoken, the Stag thrust its antlers into the Ox with such ferocity that the beast gave a groan and sank to the forest floor, dead. The Stag lifted its antlers and brayed.

"Well done, my friend," the Tailor said. "That was a mighty battle you fought."

He wondered if the old man would reappear to give the answer to the question. But instead, the Stag charged towards him and tossed the Tailor into the air with his antlers. The Tailor landed on the Stag's back, where he was forced to hang on for his life, as the creature set off running at a tremendous pace. The Tailor's eyes streamed in the wind, and his knuckles were white with clinging to the Stag's antlers. He had no idea where they were going or what path they took. He could scarcely catch his breath.

In time, they came to a ridge of rocks, where the Stag stopped. The Tailor slid from its back and lay on the ground, feeling for broken bones.

But he soon sat up at the sound of an almighty crack. The Stag was butting the rocks with its antlers over and over again until – behold! – the rocks cracked open with a blast of fire and smoke. Peering through the smoke, the Tailor saw the rocks had parted to reveal a pair of wrought-iron gates. His mouth fell open. The old man had spoken of adventure and now adventure was here.

Before he had time to think too much, the Tailor passed through the gates. He found himself in a room whose walls, ceiling and floor were all made of polished square stones. Each stone had a strange character carved into it, which glowed with an eerie light.

The Tailor inched forward into the strange room. As soon as his foot touched the stone at its centre, a grinding sound began and the whole room began to descend slowly into the earth. When at last it stopped, the whole of one wall slid open to reveal a second chamber, very much like the first. Only, where the first chamber was austere, the second was enchanting. Lights of blue, yellow and green like the lights of the Northern sky danced on its ceiling and refracted in rainbows from something inside the room. The Tailor couldn't help but go closer to investigate.

He soon found the source of the lights. A series of alcoves had been cut into the chamber wall, and each contained a glass bottle or flask. They were clearly the work of a master glass-blower. No two were alike. Some were tall and thin, some rounded like tulip bulbs, still others had circular bodies that were almost flat. Some were fluted, some had handles, some had swirls of colour captured in the plain glass, some had bubbles caught in them. As for their contents, some flasks held coloured liquids: amber, ruby, violet. Others held coloured smokes of greens and blues, surely the cause of the dancing lights. There were bottles that bubbled and foamed, others that were ice-cold to the touch. Without being told, the Tailor knew some enchantment was at work.

He then turned to two huge glass cases that almost filled the rest of the chamber. The first contained a miniature castle on a hill surrounded by woodland. Within its high stone walls were farm buildings, stables and outhouses, and beyond them rose gardens, a lake and a riding park. Every detail was perfect. Ivy grew up the stable wall. A banner with a heraldic device hung from the topmost turret. If he only had a magnifying glass, the Tailor thought, he might peep through a window to see a dais with shields hung about it, or a suckling pig turning on a spit.

But none of these wonders could hold his attention for too long, for the second glass case held the greatest wonder of all. A life-sized figure of a sleeping Girl rested on a velvet cushion. She was clad in nothing but her own yellow hair, which was so long that it covered her entirely, from head to foot. The tailor was astonished. What craftsman could have created anything so beautiful, so perfectly lifelike?

A few heartbeats later, the Tailor realised his mistake. The strands of hair about the Girl's face stirred with her breathing. This was no waxen model, but a living person! It was lucky the Tailor realised the truth when he did, for the next moment, the Girl opened her eyes and spoke:

"Who are you? If the Sorcerer has sent you, tell him I will not relent, though I lie here a thousand years."

"I know nothing about a Sorcerer." The Tailor held up his hands. "I'm just an honest Tailor caught up in an adventure. But who are you, and what are you doing in this glass coffin, so far beneath the earth?"

The Girl sighed.

"I would tell you my tale and ask you to free me, but how do I know you can be trusted? This coffin is all that keeps me from the Sorcerer's touch. He has left me without even a stitch of clothing with which to cover myself, only my hair."

"Aha!" The Tailor smiled, knowing now why the old man had given him the coat. "It is a Tailor's profession to clothe one and all. I have a garment ready for you." He took off the coat with a flourish. "As for touching you, though I marvel at your beauty, my desires do not run in that direction."

The Girl thought for a while.

"In that case, I trust you to free me. Search the coffin for a secret catch. There is one somewhere."

The Tailor searched the glass coffin until he found the catch that opened it. He pushed it back, and the lid opened with a hiss of air. He lifted it high with one hand while passing the old man's coat to the Girl with the other. He then turned his back so she could dress. When she had tied the girdle of the coat about her twice, the pair sat down on a stone bench beneath the alcoves, and the Girl told her story:

I am a noblewoman, the daughter of a rich Count. For many years after our parents died, I lived with my brother, whom I loved as my own soul. The two of us were never apart. We hunted together, played music together and took joint charge of the business of our estate. We made a vow that neither of us would ever marry but remain single and live together until the end of our days. And so it would have been, had not the Stranger arrived.

Night had fallen and a bitter storm was raging when his horse clattered into our stable-yard. He was lost, he said. A poor traveller who had been caught out between one town and the next. Could he prevail on our hospitality for a night's shelter? How could we refuse? Our parents had brought us up to think of the less fortunate before ourselves. And truly, he was a pitiful sight, with his nose raw and red, and water running off the brim of his hat.

That night, he entertained us with tales of his travels. And the next day, when the storm raged as fierce as ever, my brother persuaded him to stay a few days more. That night and the next, they sat up late playing cards and drinking brandy by the fire. I could not begrudge my brother the novelty of a male friend when our castle was so isolated, but still I went to bed with a heavy heart, missing his customary goodnight kiss. The third day, the weather broke, yet the Stranger did not leave. He and my brother rode out to hunt, leaving me alone with the rents and tithes. I confess that a bitter tear came to my eye.

That night, I lay awake on my bed, wishing the Stranger back on the road and everything returned to normal. Suddenly, I became aware of music playing, a sad and beautiful melody that conjured up the most bittersweet memories of lost childhood and golden days gone forever. I could not think from where the music came; it sounded nothing like our harpsichord or my brother's flute. I tried to get up from my bed, but to my horror, an invisible weight pressed down on my chest. It felt as though someone had laid rocks on me. Then the Stranger entered.

He was pitiable no longer. Striding through doors I had presumed locked, he loomed over my bedside. His high forehead and Grecian nose stood out in profile as shadows on the wall. His eyes were as black marbles.

"Ah, my dear." His voice purred. "You must know how I have desired you. And now you have been seduced by my music and my enchantments, there is nothing to stand in my way. Your brother believes us betrothed already." He laid a hand on the pillow.

I stiffened, willing my whole body to turn to stone.

"You shall never seduce nor take me," I said. "Nor shall any man." And I raised my voice. "Brother! Brother! Come quickly and help me!"

The Stranger gave a hiss of annoyance.

"You will regret this," he said. "There is more than one way to possess you. And you will find your brother less able to aid you once I have dealt with him."

The moment he left the room and the enchantment ceased, I leapt from the bed and pushed two chairs against the door. Next, I searched under the bed for my father's old duelling pistols. I took them from the box, loaded them and placed them on the bedside table. I then fell into an uneasy sleep.

At first light, I arose and went straight to my brother's room, meaning to tell him the truth about the Stranger. But his bed was cold and empty, as if he had not slept. I searched the castle but could find him nowhere. At last I found his manservant, who told me he had risen early to go hunting with the Stranger.

A shiver of foreboding ran down my spine. I saddled my horse, put the pistols in the pockets of my greatcoat, and galloped towards the forest with a servant following. Alas, my faithful retainer could not keep up. His horse shed a shoe and fell, so that I was left to ride alone. Even then, I suspected the Sorcerer's magic at work, for so I now knew the Stranger to be.

I pricked my horse on. Ahead of me, on a forest path, I saw the Stranger leading a Stag by a golden chain attached to a golden collar. As I wondered at this, the Stag turned its eyes on me. They were my brother's eyes, filled with tears and sorrow.

"Fiend!" I cried. "Your sorcery ends here!"

I drew my pistol and fired. But the Sorcerer put up a shield of enchantment. The bullet rebounded from his chest and pierced the head of my horse. I was thrown to the ground as the poor creature fell. The next moment, the Sorcerer stood over me. He raised his hand and spoke the words of a spell.

And so, I became as you saw me, an insensible creature encased in a glass coffin. My castle and its surroundings, he shrank to miniature form and placed in a second glass case. My servants and retainers became smokes and liquids, kept in the glass bottles you see around these walls. If I relent, he says he will restore them. But I will never relent, and evil creatures of his kind cannot enter without invitation.

But now you are here, and I am freed, though I know not how you came here.

The Tailor opened and shut his mouth several times.

"The Stag... That was the meaning of the sign! Your brother defeated the Sorcerer and brought me here to set you free." And he briefly related his adventures to the Girl."

"Then the Sorcerer's enchantments are fading," she exclaimed. "Quickly! Help me get this case and all the bottles into the open air."

Together, they lifted the second glass case into the magical lift and placed the bottles on top of it. The lift rose as slowly as it had descended. When it reached the surface, the Tailor opened the iron gates and they carried the case into the open air.

The Girl and the Tailor opened the lid of the case. With a strange popping sound, the castle and outbuildings grew by degrees until they were full-sized, and the Girl and Tailor found themselves standing in a deserted stable-yard, overlooked by a bower. The bottles and flasks stood by their feet. Wasting no time, they removed all the glass stoppers. Blue and green smokes curled into the air; amber and violet liquids spilled over the cobbles. In the blink of an eye, they were changed back to the castle's servants and retainers, and there was a great deal of laughter and back-slapping and sharing of old jokes among the liberated folk.

But the best moment came when a young man walked out of the stable leading his horse and looking so much like the Girl that the Tailor had no doubts of his identity. Then there were hugs and tears and kisses and laughter all over again. Of course, the Girl and her brother invited the Tailor to dinner. And when they had gone over the whole story and their own parts in it from every conceivable angle, the Girl said:

"Won't you come and live with us? We owe you so much, and you already feel like a friend."

"Yes, please do," said the Brother.

The Tailor paused to think. As he did, an autumn leaf fluttered past his face. He thought of the old man in the wood.

"I suppose I did do a little mending in return for shelter, after all," he said to himself.

"I'd be delighted," he said to his new family.

So, the Girl, the Brother and the Tailor lived together in harmony all their lives. None of them ever married, but they spent their days in devotion to each other. And no wicked stranger ever darkened their door again.

The Half-Marble Prince

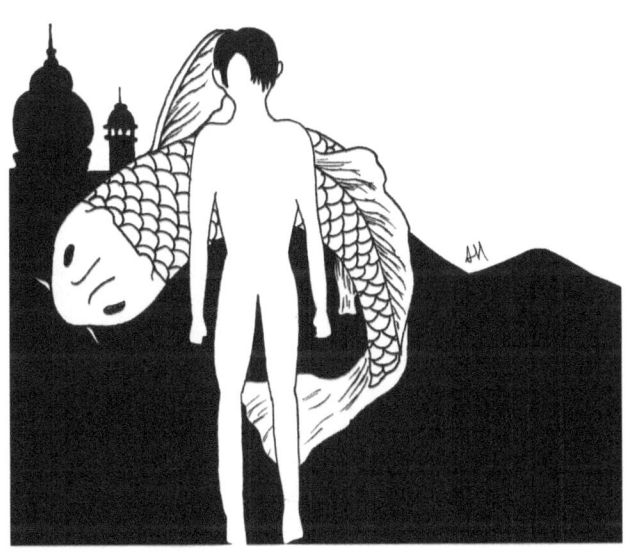

3

The Half-Marble Prince

The story of 'The Half-Marble Prince' comes from two linked tales in *The Thousand and One Nights*: 'The Fisherman and the Djinni' and a tale that has variously been told as 'The Ensorcelled Prince', 'The Young King of the Black Isles', and even 'The Semi-Petrified Prince'. It is the masculine version of 'The Glass Coffin', with which it shares various motifs. These include: the victim, their property and dependants being enchanted together by a rejected sexual partner, and a rescue achieved by a curious outsider following a mysterious trail. In this case, the victim is a Prince transformed into a semi-statue by his adulterous wife, and the rescuer a childless Sultan.

The Thousand and One Nights, also known as *The Arabian Nights*, is a collection of Arabic tales-within-tales, which has a complex, shifting history of different versions and translations almost as mysterious as some of the tales themselves. For my retelling of 'The Half-Marble Prince' I have drawn on Sir Richard Burton's 1885 English translation, as well as Moyra Caldecott's 'The Fisherman and the Genie and The King of the Ebony Isles' in *Crystal Legends* (1990). In the original tale, the wife's lover is a black slave who is described in blatantly racist terms, so I have made him simply a "rogue". The ebony ring at the end is my own addition, a finishing touch I couldn't resist.

There was once a childless Sultan who despaired of ever finding an heir. One day, as he was sitting in his palace, his vizier brought in a fisherman who wished to show the Sultan a marvel. In a certain lake, so the man said, were fish of such dazzling colour that they must be seen to be believed. To please his sovereign, the fisherman had brought one of each colour.

The fisherman held out an earthenware bowl of water in which swam four glittering fish: one white as pearl, one red as ruby, one blue as sapphire and one yellow as gold.

"This is indeed a marvel," said the Sultan. "Reward the fisherman with four hundred gold pieces and take the fish to my kitchen to be cooked. For I'll wager they taste as good as they look."

But when the fish were taken to the palace kitchen, a strange thing happened. As soon as the serving girl put them in the pan to fry, the wall of the kitchen melted away. In came a lady dressed in silks, adorned with bangles and precious jewels. She held out a wand towards the fish and said, "Fish, keep your vow!" At this, the fish sat up in the pan and said, "Yes, lady, we will." There was then a flash of blue fire, and the lady vanished through the wall, leaving the pan burned to cinders.

When the vizier heard about this, he sent for the fisherman to bring four replacement fish. But the same thing happened again. The lady appeared through the wall, saying, "Fish, keep your vow!" She then vanished in a flash of fire, leaving the pan charred to cinders.

When the same thing happened a third time, the vizier decided to tell the Sultan, and to show him the charred pan.

"There is some mystery at work here," the Sultan said. "Send for the fisherman and have him take us to the lake where he caught the fish."

So, the Sultan and his entourage of pashas and viziers, mamluks and janissaries followed the fisherman to a place none of them had ever seen before, though it lay but half a day's march from the palace. Four black hills surrounded a lake, which stood in the hollow of the valley. Peering into its crystal waters, the Sultan could see the marvellous fish of four colours, glittering in the rays of the setting sun.

The Sultan instructed his men to make camp for the night, but to his vizier he whispered a secret instruction. And so, the vizier alone knew that, when the night was deepest, the Sultan changed his clothes, girt on his sword and set out alone to solve the mystery.

After journeying three days, he came upon a black marble palace, whose gates of brass stood open and unguarded. Puzzled, the Sultan walked inside.

"Is anybody there?" he called. But the only reply was the echo of his own voice.

Going further in, the Sultan was awed by the palace's beauty. Silken curtains embroidered with gold stars hung in the doorways. Singing birds of fabulous colours flew around domed ceilings, spilling forth their song. At the centre of a courtyard, four golden lions spewed forth a fountain that looked more like cascading pearls than water. Yet nowhere could the Sultan find a single human inhabitant.

At last, he heard the sound of a man's voice, groaning and wailing. The Sultan followed the sound until he came to a chamber where a young man sat upon a couch. He was more beautiful than anyone the Sultan had seen, slim-waisted and shapely. His white forehead contrasted perfectly with his jet-black hair and ebony eyes. A beauty spot sat just above his rosy mouth.

The Sultan felt sure that the youth and the palace belonged to one another. He greeted the young man courteously, but the youth merely sighed and looked at the ground.

"Forgive me for not rising to greet you," he said, "but I am unable." And tears ran down his cheeks.

"My dear son, whatever is the matter?" the Sultan said.

Without a word, the youth drew aside the skirts of his robe.

The Sultan gasped. The young man was not sitting on a couch at all. Instead, the lower half of his body from the waist down was solid black marble. Only from the waist upwards was he a man of flesh and blood.

"In the name of God, the Merciful!" exclaimed the Sultan. "How did you come to this?"

"If you promise to help me," said the youth, "I will tell you."

The Sultan agreed, and the youth told him the following tale:

I am a Prince, the Lord of the Ebony Isles. At an early age, I was married to my cousin. In many ways, we were perfectly matched. She was beautiful and accomplished, running the women's side of the house just as I ran the men's. Many a summer's night, we would sit in the roof garden together, debating and telling tales beneath the stars. My only unease lay in matters of the bedchamber. For the sake of family honour, I tried to satisfy her, and to produce an heir, but I struggled to find the desire for the task. Often, I slept on my couch alone, in a deep sleep without dreams.

One such time, just as I was about to fall asleep, I heard one of the slaves who was fanning me say:

"Poor master! Our mistress brings shame on this house by betraying him the way she does."

"Then why does he do nothing to stop her?" said the other.

"He doesn't know," said the first. "Every night she drugs him so he cannot wake. Then she goes out into the city, to be with her lover."

These words horrified me. The next night, when she visited me as usual to debate and exchange stories, I poured away my usual drink and only pretended to drink it. I then lay on the couch and snored, as if sleeping.

"Sleep and never wake again!" I heard my wife say. "I despise you! I loathe your body! I wish I never had to live with you!"

And with that she perfumed herself, slung a sword over her shoulder, and went out into the night.

I followed at a safe distance and was disgusted to see that she made straight for the Thieves Quarter, the haunt of conjurers, beggars, alchemists, snake-charmers and every kind of rogue. From a hiding place on a nearby roof, I saw her enter the house of her lover. He was thickset, with a neck like a bull. He swept her into his arms, and they began kissing and cavorting in a way that made my stomach turn.

My anger burned so hot, I could scarcely control myself. The moment they slept, I climbed down from the roof and took up my sword, meaning to behead them both for their crime. But my stroke failed. My sword slipped from the rogue's neck, having merely wounded him. At his hissing groan, my wife awoke, and I fled across the rooftops, back to my own palace and my bed.

The next day, my wife was red-eyed and pale.

"I have suffered a great bereavement," she said. "Allow me to build a House of Lamentations in the palace courtyard, a rotunda with a dome where I can mourn my loss."

I thought the rogue must have died of his wounds in the night and gave thanks for my good fortune. My wife had the rotunda built and put it about that her parents and brothers had perished in a tragic accident. I alone knew for whom she really mourned.

Every day, my wife went to the House of Lamentations in the courtyard. I hoped in time that her visits would lessen, and we would resume our starlit debates, but it was not so. Indeed, she seemed to spend more time in the rotunda than anywhere else.

Eventually, I said to her:

"Light of my eyes, can we not resume our friendship and go on as we once did? I have borne with this mourning for a long while, but it is time to forget and return to your husband."

The scorn from her eyes was like fire.

"Husband! When have you ever been my husband? I have only one husband on this earth, and by God, I will see him restored to me!"

She fled into the House of Lamentations, and I followed at her heels. Beneath the echoing cupola, she fell upon a couch and kissed the mouth of her roguish lover. All this time, he had not been dead but merely injured in the throat. All around the couch, I could see potions and snake skins, incense and texts in strange scripts. She was trying by magic arts to restore her lover to full health.

The rage I had long buried rose to my throat.

"Adulteress!" I screamed. "Witch! I bore with your grief patiently, thinking you would return to me. But all the time, you have been keeping your lover in the heart of my palace. By God, I will finish what I started!"

Again, I took up my sword. But my wife had learned well from the sorcerers with whom she kept company. She thrust out her hand towards me and said:

"I curse you! From now on, you will be half man and half marble, unable to leave your palace or move from the spot. Your beloved Ebony Isles will shrink to black hills around a lake. Your subjects will become fish: the Muslims white, the Zoroastrians red, the Jews yellow and the Christians blue. And you will suffer. Oh yes, my lord, you will suffer!"

The Prince looked at the Sultan with tears in his eyes.

"Every morning, she comes to this chamber. She strips me to the waist and gives me a hundred lashes with the whip. My wounds never heal. I am in torment every day."

The Sultan passed a hand over his eyes.

"Where is she now?"

"As soon as she has finished scourging me," said the Prince, "she goes to the House of Lamentations. It is still here in my courtyard. She spends all her time there, feeding her lover, keeping him alive by her magic arts. But I believe the fellow is no more alive than I am. All I hear from the courtyard are wordless groans."

"Very well, then," said the Sultan. "I know what I must do."

The next time his wife came to scourge the Prince, the Sultan sneaked into the House of Lamentations. There lay the lover, more dead than alive. With a swift blow of his sword, the Sultan ended his misery. After disposing of the body in a well, he lay on the couch and covered himself with the coverlet.

The wife soon came in with a bowl of meat broth and a goblet of wine.

"Eat and drink, light of my eyes," she said, and sighed. "Alas that with all my arts I cannot heal your wound! Oh, how I wish you would speak to me!"

This was the Sultan's opportunity. In a hoarse voice, he said:

"My heart's delight, I cannot be well until you reverse the spell you cast on your husband. That is why your efforts have failed."

"You spoke!" cried the wife. "This is indeed a sign from heaven. I will do as you say."

She went out into the palace and took from her chamber a metal bowl. This she filled with water and set it to boil, casting into it magic powders, and speaking secret words. Then she sprinkled the water over the enchanted Prince, saying:

"I revoke the curse! Be as you were before, a man of flesh and blood!"

Instantly, the Prince felt the marble begin to soften. His legs shook and trembled and he fell to the floor, kissing it and looking in wonder at his new legs.

"Now leave my sight before I kill you!" said the wife and turned on her heels.

When she reached the House of Lamentations, she knelt by the couch and asked the Sultan if he was improved.

"A little," the Sultan croaked. "But for me to be truly well, you must restore your husband's realm and subjects."

So, the wife went back to the metal bowl and said more words. She then sprinkled water in the direction of the lake. The instant she did so, the lake expanded to a vast inland sea. The four hills became islands, forested with trees of ebony. The fish rose and stood upright, turning again into citizens of four faiths. The bazaars were thronged with people buying and selling, the places of worship murmured with prayer. And at the centre of the city, raised on a hill, stood the palace of black marble with its gates of brass.

The wife hurried back to the House of Lamentations to see if her lover was well.

"Come close and kiss me," whispered the Sultan, "and you will see."

So, the wife leaned close to kiss her supposed lover. As soon as she was close enough, the Sultan leapt from his couch and clove her in two with his sword. A greenish smoke and a foul smell arose from the body. She was a witch indeed.

The Sultan returned to the Prince, who was now on his feet, and walking about the palace in a daze of wonder. When he saw the Sultan, he knelt and kissed the older man's hand.

"How can I thank you," he said. "for all you have done?"

The Sultan plucked his moustache.

"It would honour me greatly if you would become my son and heir. But you have a realm of your own here. I couldn't possibly ask..."

The Prince clasped the Sultan's hands.

"Nothing you could have said would make me happier. This realm has too many bitter memories. I will leave it to my brother, who already has children. And I will go with you, my Father. Since you rescued me, I never want to be parted from you in this life."

So, the Prince went with the Sultan. The journey back took much longer now that the Ebony Isles were disenchanted and in their proper place. They journeyed with an escort of mamluks bringing ebony, pearls and singing birds as gifts for the Prince's new realm. People cheered in the streets when the Sultan came home, and the vizier rushed out to meet him with tears in his eyes. He had feared he would never see the Sultan again.

When the Sultan got home, he did not forget to reward the fisherman, whose gift had begun the whole adventure. He instated the disenchanted Prince as his heir and lived happily, no longer lonely and childless.

As for the Prince, the only reminder of his strange enchantment was an ebony ring that he wore on his right hand. If ever memories or bad dreams came to trouble him, he would look at it and remember how a Sultan came to find him in the marble palace and set him free to be who he was born to be.

The Tale of Princess Kaguya

4

The Tale of Princess Kaguya

Another tale of a childless father finding a child, only this time the discovery of a daughter is just the beginning of the story.

'The Tale of Princess Kaguya' is a beloved Japanese folk tale, which has been retold many times, including as an animated film by Studio Ghibli in 2013. It was first written down for English-speaking readers in 1903 by Yei Theodora Ozaki in her *Japanese Fairy Book* (where it is called 'The Bamboo-Cutter and the Moon-Child'). Ms Ozaki was a Japanese-English aristocrat and friend of Andrew Lang, who encouraged her to write her book of fairy tales. Like the heroine of this tale, she was a child of two cultures who refused the marriages her father tried to arrange for her.

'The Tale of Princess Kaguya' illustrates the tragic consequences of family and friends failing to understand a person's identity. It leaves the reader with a bittersweet ending, which most Western fairy tales do not have.

There was once an old bamboo-cutter who lived on the edge of a forest. Every day, he would go into the forest to cut bamboo, and every night he would go home to his hut and his aged wife, his only companion in this world. They had no children and no grandchildren, and this made them very sad. But they had long since buried the sadness deep in their hearts, knowing it was now too late for things to change.

One day, the old man went into the forest as usual. As he approached a clump of bamboo, he noticed a strange light shining from it, as if the moon had fallen to earth and was shining its light in the grove. Intrigued, he went closer. The light seemed to be coming from one particular stem of bamboo. Taking his knife, he cut carefully into the stem. Moonlight pooled into the grove. There, in the centre of the bamboo stalk, was a tiny little girl, only three inches high. She was perfectly formed and exquisitely beautiful, with raven hair and skin like pearls.

"This must be a gift from heaven," the old man exclaimed.

Carefully, he carried the bamboo-child home and showed her to his wife.

"A gift from heaven, indeed," said the wife. "We will love her always."

The old man and his wife raised the bamboo-child as if she were their own. She soon grew to a usual size, and they marvelled at her beauty and quickness of understanding. Every day, some new thing she said or did brought them delight. She brought the old woman flowers she had picked and sat on the old man's lap as he told stories of an evening. The couple felt quite young again and could hardly remember life before their daughter arrived.

In addition, another miracle occurred. The first week after finding his daughter, the old man was again cutting bamboo in the forest, when he noticed the same light he had seen before. Cutting into the bamboo, he discovered inside the stem a shining pile of gold nuggets.

"Heaven is providing for the daughter we were sent," he told his wife when he brought it home. And the wife agreed.

A week or two later, the same thing happened again. The next month, he cut into the bamboo to discover a hoard of precious stones. Soon, he was no longer a poor bamboo-cutter. In fact, he gave up bamboo cutting all together, and began to live the life of a nobleman. He had a beautiful house built with covered walkways, a courtyard garden and its own bath-house. Servants brought the best of seasonal food to the family's table. They dressed in silk kimonos and spotless white stockings, and the old man travelled to visit his neighbours in a lacquered *kago*, or sedan-chair.

As for the daughter, she was kept behind screens like a princess, hidden from the vulgar eyes of the world. She was taught calligraphy, poetry and how to play the koto. When she came of age, a prestigious name-giver bestowed upon her the name Princess Kaguya, a name meaning "the shining light of the moon". For that was how everyone felt when they were in her presence: as if the moon had shone its gentle light on them.

The celebrations following Princess Kaguya's naming went on for three days. There were fireworks, music, wrestling and poetry competitions. The fame of Princess Kaguya's beauty and accomplishment spread from family and friends out into the town. There was no one to compare to her, they said, not in all the eight islands. And still her fame spread, from town to town and from province to province, until young men fell in love just at the mention of Princess Kaguya's name. Suitors gathered outside the house and made little holes in the fence, hoping to catch a glimpse of the Princess. Even the hem of her kimono or the breath of her perfume would be enough, they said. But the old man guarded his daughter jealously. No servant could be bribed, no wall could be breached. In the end, only five suitors remained.

These men stood outside the house day and night, come sun, rain or snow. They were samurai, all of them, trained in steadfastness and honour. Nothing would deter them from their quest to meet with Princess Kaguya. They sent her poetry about their sleeves being red with tears of blood. They picked the first cherry blossoms, the first ripe persimmons to send to her, in hopes of winning her heart. And when all that failed, they sat in silent vigil, their legs crossed like monks, waiting for her to reply.

The old man, meanwhile, had begun to pity the five suitors. They were worthy men, samurai, of good families. Any one of them would be a worthy match for his daughter. But whenever he broached the subject with her, she refused to listen.

"Father, I know you and Mother have been so good and kind to me all these years. I would do anything to make you happy, but not this. I have no desire to marry; it is not in my nature."

"As I'm not your real father, I cannot compel you," the ex-bamboo-cutter said. "But consider how your mother and I are getting on in years. How will you live when we are gone? A good marriage will give you security. Besides, these men have been waiting at our gate through one season after another. Will you not take pity on them?"

And her father went on to describe all that the suitors had been through, standing steadfastly in the snow, meditating throughout the night, all in the hopes of meeting her. When she heard the tale, Princess Kaguya felt truly sorry for the men.

"I will see them," she said, "but you must allow me to dictate what follows."

The old man would do anything for his marvellous daughter, so he invited the suitors to come into the house. They could hardly contain their excitement at the thought of an audience with the famed Princess Kaguya. Though she sat behind a curtain as they knelt on the wooden floor, the merest glimpse of her shadow was a thrill to them, and the sound of her voice had them in ecstasies.

"Gentlemen, my father has told me about your suit and your long vigil. Though I fear your wait is in vain, I will give each of you a chance to prove your love for me. If any man can succeed in the quest I give him, I will consent to be his wife."

The suitors tensed in anticipation. Their moment of deliverance was at hand.

"Each of you must seek the precious object I name. As there are five of you, the objects represent the five elements that make up this world. You, sir," (and she named the first suitor) "are to bring me the stone bowl of the Buddha, which is said to be in India."

The first man quaked at such a task, but the Princess went on to name the second suitor's quest:

"You, sir, are to go to the Mountain of Horai in the Eastern Sea. On its summit grows a tree with branches of gold, leaves of silver and jewelled fruits. You are to bring me a branch of this tree."

Each of the tasks was similarly impossible. The third man was to go to China and bring back the skin of the Fire Rat, which was completely flame-proof.

The fourth man was to seek out the Dragon of the Sea. On its neck was a jewel that glowed with five colours. He was to capture this jewel and bring it back to the Princess.

The fifth man was to bring back the swallow's cowrie shell, which it had carried in its stomach for a year, and then hidden in its high nest.

"Gentlemen, these are your tasks and I wish you luck in them," said Princess Kaguya, and the suitors were dismissed.

At first, they despaired of even attempting such tasks. They were impossible, the stuff of dreams and tales! But at last one of them said:

"Gentlemen, are we not samurai? Which of us has ever backed down when facing adversity? To do so would bring shame on ourselves and on our families. I, for one, am willing to attempt the Princess's quest."

At this, the other four declared likewise. They each went their separate ways to seek out the fabled treasures.

Not a word was heard of the suitors for three years. The Princess and her parents lived contentedly at home as they had always done, although they sometimes wondered what had become of the five samurai. Then one day, the first of them returned.

He was carrying something wrapped in cloth of gold. When he unwrapped it before the veiled Princess, everyone could see that it was a stone bowl.

"Princess, this is the stone begging bowl of the Buddha himself, brought all the way from India." He bowed with his head to the floor.

Behind her curtain, Princess Kaguya smiled.

"I doubt that, sir," she said. "If this were truly the Buddha's bowl, it would shine with immortal light. This is just an ordinary temple bowl."

Ashamed, the man confessed it was true. He had no idea how to even get to India, never mind finding the Buddha's bowl. So, he had persuaded a temple in Kyoto to sell him this one, then waited a suitable amount of time before bringing it to the Princess.

"I'm sorry," he said. "It was only my great love for you that made me act thus."

The next to arrive was the suitor who had been sent to seek the jewelled branch of Mount Horai. He arrived in great style, and had his servants set down a large plant pot, in which was planted what looked to be a cutting from a tree. It glittered gold and silver in the sunlight, and jewels gleamed from its branches.

"Princess, I have journeyed long and hard to bring you a branch from the Tree of Mount Horai," he said. "When last I left your presence, I took a ship to the Eastern Sea in search of the treasure. Oh, the things I endured! A storm engulfed us, so terrible that it threatened to tear the boards asunder. For ten days and nights, we never saw the light of the sun. The storm ran us aground on an island inhabited by demons. Only my diplomacy saved us from being killed and eaten. The demons helped us mend the boat and we set sail once more, only to be tossed by high waves and then becalmed for two weeks, so we almost died from thirst. At last we came to land on an island with a high mountain at its centre, and on the mountain peak, a shining light.

"Is this Mount Horai?" I asked the first man I saw. He glowed with light, looking more like a spirit than a man.

"Indeed, it is," he said. "The blessed Mount Horai, where stands the golden tree."

"With great difficulty, I ascended the summit of the mountain and set eyes upon the marvellous tree. I reached out my hand..."

At that point, there was a commotion in the gardens outside. The old man called a servant to slide open the door and see what was going on. Outside were six jewellers from the local guild. They bore staves in their hands and spoke to the servant angrily.

"That samurai lord you have in there ordered us to make that jewelled tree three years ago. For three years, we have worked day and night, turning down all other custom. And now it is finished, he refuses to pay us."

Princess Kaguya could not resist a little laugh at the comical outcome. The jewellers were duly paid, but the second suitor was dismissed in disgrace. It wasn't long before he retired to a monastery, leaving worldly society altogether.

Next came the suitor who had been sent to find the skin of the Fire Rat. He was very confident that the article was genuine and told the Princess so.

"In that case, you won't object if we test it by throwing it into the fire?" she said.

"By all, means, go ahead," said the suitor. "A learned friend brought me this all the way from China. And believe me, it wasn't cheap."

At that, a servant tossed the skin into the brazier. There was a horrible crackling sound and an acrid smell. The room filled with smoke.

"The Fire Rat skin!" cried the suitor. "No! No! Make it stop! I've been cheated! Cheated!"

And so, he had, but as he had no other Fire Rat skin to produce, he was dismissed, a failure.

The fourth suitor did not return in person, but instead sent a manservant to say that he was ill in bed with a dreadful cold and fever. After sending men near and far to enquire after the Sea Dragon and its jewel, he had decided there was nothing for it but to go to sea himself. The captain of the ship he took thought he was crazy, but nevertheless had taken the suitor's money and embarked with him on the quest. It was hurricane season, and the winds and tides were against them from the start. They were blown here and there, with waves washing overboard and men clinging to the ropes for their lives. At one point, the suitor thought he saw a Sea Dragon. It was lithe and terrible, and rocked the boat until it almost capsized. But the captain told him that he was in a fever, and what he had seen had merely been the crests of the waves. At any rate, said the servant, his master had returned home extremely unwell and with no intention of courting the Princess further.

News of the fifth suitor was even worse. He had climbed a high cliff, where he believed the swallow had made a nest for the magical cowrie shell. But in attempting to reach for it, he had slipped and fallen to his death.

All further talk was silenced by the death of the fifth suitor. He had been a noble man, and Princess Kaguya mourned his senseless death.

"Why would he go so far on an impossible quest?" She said. "Surely, now men will leave me alone."

And indeed, most men did leave her alone, for the tale of the five suitors had spread, and most feared the consequences, should they dare to court Princess Kaguya.

But there was one man who, hearing of Princess Kaguya, decided he must know her, whatever the cost. That man was the Emperor of Japan. The Princess intrigued him deeply. What was it about her that made men die for her love, even though she refused to be wooed? What was she really like, this woman that everyone adored, yet no one really seemed to know? As Emperor, he knew what it was to hide behind bamboo curtains, worshipped as a god and forbidden to be looked upon. Perhaps he and this Princess Kaguya were not so very different? Perhaps he could get to know her.

He arranged to take a hunting party to the countryside where the Princess and her parents lived, still close to the bamboo forest where she had been found. The Emperor soon outrode his retinue and reached the house alone. Peering through the hole in the fence where once the suitors had looked, he caught a glimpse of black hair and layers of autumn-coloured kimono. He removed a few stalks of bamboo and squeezed through the gap. There before him was the beautiful maiden, her eyes bright black against her white skin. When she saw him, she flinched, and her skin began to shine with unbearable brightness. The Emperor covered his eyes.

"Forgive me. I never meant to startle you or cause you any fear." The Emperor's voice was gentle, as if coaxing a shy fawn. "I only wished to visit you and offer my friendship. I am the Emperor of these islands."

"Please, Your Majesty, don't make me say anything traitorous," said Princess Kaguya. "I cannot become your wife or enter the inner seraglio. I know you have the authority to command anyone under your lordship, but I am not... No, I've said too much."

"In truth, there's nothing I'd like more than to bring you to my palace, where I might see you every day," said the Emperor. "But I will not force you. Please, let us sit and talk for a while, before people begin searching for us."

They sat in the garden and talked, the Emperor all the while falling more and more in love. Princess Kaguya was more than just a beauty or a woman of refinement. She had intelligence and insight beyond his own. And something else. An air that was somehow...beyond this world.

When the Emperor left, Princess Kaguya agreed that they might write to each other. And from that day, they wrote often, exchanging poetry and observations on nature. From time to time, the Emperor became emboldened to speak of his love. But the reply was always the same: those feelings could never be requited.

"Please do not ask me again," she wrote in her last letter. "For I feel a great change coming over me, and it may be that our correspondence will soon come to an end."

What could she mean? The Emperor puzzled over her words, greatly troubled. Her foster-parents were worried, too. Lately, the Princess had taken to gazing out at the moon for long periods of time. Sometimes they would see tears on her cheek or hear her softly weeping.

At last, her father asked her what was wrong.

"You have always known there was something different about me," she said. "I have always known it too, although I was never quite sure what it was. But now I'm certain. Father, I'm not of this earth. I'm a Moon Princess. I was sent to be reborn on this earth for a time, but now it is time to me to return to the moon and to my people, among whom

I can exercise my true nature. They will come for me at the next full moon, on the fifteenth day of August."

"No!" Her father was distraught. "It cannot be. You cannot leave us. What about the Emperor?"

"I will write to him," she said, "and tell him what must happen."

The old man bristled.

"I will write to him myself. He will be able to stop this from happening."

"No, Father, you mustn't try to stop it," the Princess pleaded. "This is my true nature. I *am* a Princess of the Moon."

But her father refused to listen. He wrote to the Palace, informing the Emperor of what the Moon People intended to do. As he had expected, the Emperor was horrified. He sent two thousand warriors to guard the house on the night of the fifteenth of August: a thousand on the roof and a thousand at the gates. Their quivers were filled with arrows and their bows were strung and ready.

"It will do no good," Princess Kaguya said to her mother. "Their weapons won't work on the People of the Moon or stop them from taking me. But Father and the Emperor won't listen." Tears came to her eyes. "I wish I didn't have to leave you all; I love you so much. But it's time for me to go."

The old woman hugged her close and they wept together as the night wore on and the soldiers kept watch.

In the early hours of the morning, a cloud crossed the moon. It seemed at first as though it was just drifting by, but gradually it grew closer, and those watching began to hear music coming from it.

"It's them," said Princess Kaguya. "They're coming for me."

The cloud drew closer. All could now see a flying chariot on top of the cloud with a radiant being inside it, the King of the Moon. Around him stood shining beings with wings, playing many kinds of instruments.

"The time has come," said the Moon King. "Bamboo-cutter, we thank you and your wife for your care of our daughter. But now she must return to us and fully become a Moon Princess once more."

"No, you cannot take her! You mustn't. Captains, tell your men to fire!"

The soldiers loosed their arrows, but it did neither good nor harm. In mid-air, they all turned to flowers and fell harmlessly to earth.

"Father, don't fight." Princess Kaguya had come out of the house and stood before the silver cloud. "We have had so many happy years together. Let it not end in bitterness."

"Come, Princess Kaguya," said the Moon King. "Let us not waste any more time. Step up to this cloud. Your sisters are waiting to put a cloak of feathers around your shoulders. Once it is upon you, you will forget all the troubles of this world. And when you drink from the Elixir of Life, which they will give you, you will become truly immortal and able to live on the moon."

The Moon King held out his hand. Princess Kaguya took it and stepped onto the floating cloud. She took a sip of the Elixir of Life and was about to let the shining beings put the cloak on her shoulders, when —"Wait! I have forgotten my friend, the Emperor. Let me quickly write him a note to say goodbye before I lose my human form."

In spite of the Moon King's impatience, everyone waited while she wrote her last words to the Emperor. She wrapped the letter around the vial containing the last drops of the Elixir of Life and bade the Captain of the Guard take it to His Majesty.

At last she said, "I am ready. Goodbye, Mother and Father. Do not forget me, though I forget you."

They put the cloak of feathers on her shoulders. At once it grew into wings, which she stretched out as the cloud began to rise. The music began playing once more, and the old people watched it recede with tears in their eyes, until it was nothing but a speck on the surface of the moon.

In a pool of silver moonlight, the guards dispersed and returned to the palace, taking the letter with them. When the Emperor read it, he was silent for many days. Then, with its words burned on his heart forever, he commanded his ministers to take the letter - along with the Elixir of Life, which he dared not touch - to the top of Mount Fuji. There they burned together, and there they are burning still on the peak of the sacred mountain.

Zellandine and Troylus

5

Zellandine and Troylus

For some asexuals, reconciling a desire for parenthood with a lack of desire – or even repulsion – for the sexual act can be a difficult struggle.

'Zellandine and Troylus' is one of the earliest-known versions of 'Sleeping Beauty' and comes from the medieval French romance *Perceforest* (c.1330–44). It also has echoes of 'Rapunzel', as the maiden is kept in a tower that can only be accessed by a high window. Many commentators find the tale deeply problematic because of its apparent portrayal of non-consensual sex. But viewed on a symbolic level, it can be read as a story about the wish to absent during sex and childbirth. I have never forgotten a dream I had as a teenager, in which I became pregnant because of a dream. In the inner dream, the act was somehow honourable, but in the outer dream I felt only shame and fear. 'Zellandine and Troylus' seems to speak to that same anxiety.

Another thing I like about 'Zellandine and Troylus' is that, while Zellandine's father views her condition as an "illness", we are told it was ordained by the gods at her birth. For anyone who has suffered "cures" for asexuality, it is good to be reminded that it is not an illness. We were just born this way.

My retelling is based on an English translation by Susan McNeill Cox (1990).

The Fates never stop spinning. Three goddesses: one to draw out the thread of life, one to twist it, one to cut it off. People said Zellandine's long sleep was an illness, but it was her destiny, spun at her birth by three goddesses: Lucina, Venus and Themis, who preside over life, love and destiny. They were present at her naming-day, present on the island of Zelland, where the Temple of the Three Goddesses stood. And though she did not see them, they were present when her life took its unique twist of fate.

It began with her betrothal to the knight, Troylus. Troylus the noble, Troylus whom she saw in her dreams, Troylus whose sweet-scented babies she could almost feel in her arms. There was nothing she wanted more than to wed Troylus. And yet. And yet...

Troylus was away in his own country of Scotland when he first heard of Zellandine's illness. A ship arrived, having been blown off course. The knights aboard were hoping to make land in the realm of the Britons, there to seek Zellandin, brother of Zellandine. His sister was gravely ill.

Troylus' heart missed a beat.

"What is the matter with her? I am Zellandine's betrothed husband and have been seeking news of her for many moons."

"It seems she was staying with some maidens," the knights said, "when she fell into a deep sleep. Since that time, she has not awoken. She neither eats nor drinks, except that which can be forced into her."

"And what do her doctors say?" Troylus asked.

"The doctors have neither explanation nor cure. That is why we are seeking Zellandin," the knights said.

"Then seek no more, I pray you," said Troylus. "Do not wait for Zellandin but take me with you to Zelland My father was a doctor, and it may be that I can bring healing to my beloved Zellandine."

They set sail, and soon arrived on the island. A high wind forced him to take refuge in a local manor house, where the lady of the manor told him more of Zellandine's strange illness:

"She had gone to Britain to attend a party in honour of King Perceforest. After the feast, she stayed on with her cousins and other young ladies. It so happened that she took a flax distaff from the hand of her cousin and began to spin. But as soon as she did so, she fell into a swoon from which she never awoke. From that time to this, she has slept without eating or drinking, but losing neither colour nor weight. It is said the goddess Venus takes care of her."

When Troylus heard this, he was even more determined to find the place where Zellandine lay. Unfortunately, the lady of the manor had a son who was also in love with Princess Zellandine. She drugged Troylus, so the next morning he woke up dazed, not knowing who he was or what he was doing. In his confused state, he wandered across the island until, as Fate would have it, he arrived at the palace of Zelland, home of Zellandine's father. When people saw his unkempt beard and staring eyes, they called him a madman and a fool. But King Zelland's actual Fool cried out:

"This is no madman! This is the man who will cure Zellandine."

So, the King took Troylus with him to the Temple of the Three Goddesses, where he daily prayed to Venus for his daughter's recovery. There, in front of Venus' statue, Troylus fell asleep. In his dream, he saw Zellandine, wandering lost and confused as he had done. Their eyes met, and it seemed to him that she was begging for help.

Suddenly, Troylus awoke. The goddess Venus herself was anointing his eyes. For a moment he saw her, beautiful and terrible. Then the temple guard was leaning over him, shaking him to wakefulness.

"I remember it all now!" Troylus said. "I came here to cure Princess Zellandine."

"Ah, that's a sad case," said the guard. "Although I think it was fated to happen. I remember how the baby Princess was brought to this temple, eight days after her birth. Food and drink were laid out for the Three Goddesses, to invite them to come and spin the child's fate. Each place setting had a golden plate, goblet and knife, but the knife of Themis had fallen to the floor. When the three heavenly queens descended, Lucina, goddess of childbirth blessed the newborn with good health. But Themis, annoyed by the loss of her knife, destined that when Zellandine was old enough to be betrothed, a splinter would pierce her finger while she was spinning flax, and this would cause an endless sleep. Venus, goddess of love replied that she would find a cure to this fate. And that is the true cause of Zellandine's illness."

"I thank you for your help, good man," said Troylus. "But can you tell me where the Princess lies sleeping?"

"Certainly, sir," said the man. "She lies in a place called Jumel Castle, at the top of a tall tower. There her father has placed her, in the care of the gods."

Troylus set off across the island to seek Jumel Castle. He didn't know which way to take, as the country was wild and barren. On his second day of riding, he saw a shrine to Venus and knelt down to pray. He prayed long and hard that he would be able to find Zellandine and cure her. As the sun set, he thought he heard a female voice speaking to him:

"Noble knight, do not lose heart. If you are steadfast, you will find your way into the tower where your love lies sleeping. When you get there, you must go through the opening to find the fruit that provides the remedy."

Troylus thanked Lady Venus for her help. The next day he rode out once more. Against the sparse horizon, the castle soon stood out. When he got close, he saw there were two tall towers, one at each end of the castle. He didn't know which one housed his beloved Zellandine, but he rode until he came close to one of the towers. To his dismay, he saw it was surrounded by a moat with a drawbridge. The bridge was drawn up and there was no other way across. The tower was extraordinarily high, and every single door and window had been bricked up except for one, right at the top of the tower on the eastern side.

A messenger came out of the main gate of the castle.

"Tell me, is this the tower where Princess Zellandine sleeps?" Troylus asked him.

"It is indeed, sir."

"But how might one enter?" Troylus said. "Is there no other way in or out apart from that window."

"There is not," said the man. "All other entrances are walled up, except this window, which is the entrance for the gods."

Troylus' heart sank. A window for the gods! How could a mortal man go through? And yet Venus had promised him that he was the one to achieve this quest. He led his horse away from the castle, tied it to a tree stump and sat down to think. There must be a way in. He could cross the moat but...what then? He almost felt like giving up, but then he thought about Zellandine, his adored Zellandine. He was nothing in this world without her. He had loved her ever since she had sent him a wondrous gift, a crown of nine golden letters. He could not leave her trapped in the tower.

He went back to the tower and, without further thought, jumped into the moat. The chill almost took his breath, but he swam on through reeds and duckweed until he came to the other side. He scrambled to his feet and began walking round and round the tower. Its sides were as smooth as if they had been polished. In vain, he looked for the slightest chink in which he could gain a foothold.

"What am I to do?" he thought.

At that moment, he heard a sound behind him like a whirlwind. And when he looked behind, he saw a handsome youth standing on the other side of the moat. With a smile on his face and not the slightest flinch, the youth walked across the moat as if it were a stone bridge.

"Who on earth are you?" Troylus exclaimed.

"That is not for me to say," the youth answered. "It is enough for you to know that I am here to help you. I can get you into the tower as easily as I crossed this moat, and back out again, too. Only you must follow my instructions."

"If you can do all that, it will be the greatest wonder I ever saw, and I'll be only too glad to do as you say," Troylus said.

"Very well, then. In a moment, you will climb upon my back and I will take you to the window. Once inside the tower, you will follow the advice of the goddess Venus. At midnight, go to the window and I will bring you safely back to earth."

Troylus readily agreed to the youth's terms. He climbed upon the youth's back. To his astonishment, the youth was instantly transformed to an enormous bird, with feathers of gold and burning red. It flew to the top of the tower and let Troylus in through the window, before flying away again.

Troylus looked about the room. A lamp was softly burning, hanging by a silver chain. It illuminated a four-poster bed, piled high with snowy white pillows. The curtains were pure white with threads of silver. In the bed, sleeping beneath silver-white coverlets, was Zellandine. Her cheeks had a delicate blush, her chest gently rose and fell. She looked more like a maiden taking a refreshing nap than someone suffering a grave illness. Troylus couldn't help but feel his blood warm at the sight of her; he had not seen her in many months and she was even more desirable than he remembered.

He found a candle in a silver candlestick on a trunk at the foot of the bed. He lit it from the lamp, drew closer to the bed and sat down. Ah! How beautiful she was! He traced the line of her brow with his finger, smoothing back her auburn hair. She made not a stir. Softly, he stroked her cheek, touched her lips with feather-light fingertips. Nothing. Tears came to his eyes. There lay his love, white as the lily, red as the rose, yet insensible.

"Oh, my love!" he sighed. "What has brought you to this? Why do you not wake? I have missed you so much, longed to hold you in my arms. But now that we are finally alone together, you cannot speak to me or respond in any way. Forgive me, my love, but it angers and upsets me to be thus cheated of all we might have enjoyed."

Still Zellandine slept on.

"Are you in there, my love?" Troylus wept. "In my dream you seemed to look on me with love and beg my help. Will you feel it if I kiss you?"

He bent his head over hers and placed a tender kiss on her forehead. Then, suddenly emboldened, he kissed her eyelids, her cheeks, her lips, her throat. More than twenty times he kissed her, and yet she did not stir. Troylus' tears sparkled on her cheeks like diamonds and trickled in crystal rivers towards her pillows.

"Venus, what must I do?" he cried. "You promised me I would enter this tower, and I have. But what good is that when my love lies insensible? You said that love would lead me to the opening where lies the fruit that will cure this maiden. But I don't know how to find it. I don't know where that plant grows. Venus, don't leave me like this!"

The curtains of the bed softly stirred, and a voice whispered in Troylus' ear:

"Are you really such a fool as those at Zelland believed you to be? Follow your desire. The lady dreams of becoming a wife and mother. Give her the gift she longs for."

Troylus flushed red.

"In her sleep?" he said, aghast. "Without her permission?"

"She gives her permission, trust me," said Venus. "Now, do as you are bidden."

In truth, Troylus would have been hard pressed to resist, for the flames of desire had arisen in him. He took off his clothes and got under the covers, where Zellandine lay completely unclothed, white and tender. Troylus was overcome with love and happiness. If only Zellandine could have spoken or responded in some way, his joy would have been even greater. As gently as his ardour would allow, he caressed her until at last he planted his seed in her. At that, she gave a heavy sigh, and Troylus felt she knew what they had done. He lay back on the bed and drifted in and out of sleep, until he heard a whirr of wings at the window.

"Hurry and get dressed," came the voice of the handsome youth. "It is time to leave."

"Already?" Troylus was forlorn. As he struggled into his clothes, he looked at the bed, expecting to see Zellandine wake, but she did not stir.

"Hurry!" said the youth again.

Troylus stood by the bed one last time and took Zellandine's hand. She was wearing the ring he had given for their betrothal. Quickly, he slipped the ring from her finger and exchanged it for his own betrothal ring, placing Zellandine's ring on his finger.

"My dear and perfect friend," he whispered. "I am leaving now because I must, but I will return to you."

Then he climbed on the back of the bird-youth, and they flew away into the night.

Troylus' visit to the tower had not gone unnoticed. Zellandine's father the King was looking out of his window and noticed that the light from the tower was unusually bright. Unbeknown to Troylus, he had his own way of visiting his daughter, by means of an underground passage that led to the tower's ground floor. This was the way he now took. When he had climbed the stairs to the top floor, he tried the door of Zellandine's room, only to find it locked.

"Can it be that the gods have visited her?" he asked himself.

He went to wake his sister, a woman whose opinion he had always trusted, and together they returned to the tower. Peering through a crack in the wall around the door, they were amazed at what they saw. A knight in full armour stood by the window with his back to them. On the windowsill sat an enormous bird with feathers of gold and burning red. The knight climbed on the bird's back and together they flew away.

"It must have been Mars, the god of war, who has visited my daughter," said the King, and his sister agreed.

The King unlocked the door and they crept into the room. There lay Zellandine in the bed, a candle burning low at her bedside. The King thought she looked more flushed than usual, although her expression was peaceful.

"Do you think Mars could have given her some medicine?" the King asked his sister.

"If that is the case, she will soon be cured," the sister answered. "But I will watch over her in the meantime and visit her every day by means of the passage you have shown me."

The King's sister did as she had promised. Every day, she visited Zellandine in her tower. She washed Zellandine's face, plumped up her pillows and fed her a tiny sip of goat's milk from a bowl, the only food she could get the girl to take. For although she had told her brother she agreed with his observations, as a woman she had her own ideas about what Mars was doing with her niece. Her suspicions were confirmed as the months went by and Zellandine's belly began to swell. In all, nine months passed, until one night Zellandine was delivered of a handsome baby. Her aunt assisted in the delivery, cut the cord and took away the afterbirth, and through all this Zellandine slumbered still.

"Won't you wake, my sweet girl?" the aunt pleaded. "You have a beautiful baby boy. Won't you open your eyes and see him?"

She wrapped the baby in swaddling and placed him next to his mother. Straight away, the baby began suckling with his mouth, looking for his mother's milk. Instead, he found his mother's little finger, which nevertheless he sucked eagerly. A moment later, he began coughing.

"Oh dear, what's the matter? Has baby got wind?" said the aunt.

She picked him up and patted him on the back. At that, he coughed out the splinter that had been lodged in his mother's finger. The next moment, Zellandine gave a murmur and opened her eyes. The aunt cried for joy:

"My dear child, you are awake! Praise be to Mars, and to Venus, who always swore to restore you!"

Zellandine rubbed her eyes.

"What dreams I have had! I dreamt the moon came in at my window and I became pregnant and gave birth to Troylus' child."

The aunt smiled through her tears and placed the baby in Zellandine's arms.

"You do have a child, my love. See! But no mortal man such as Troylus could be the father. That is impossible. The father of your child is Mars, who came in at the window of the gods."

At this, Zellandine began to wail.

"No! No! It was Troylus. It had to be Troylus. How could a god come in and take what I have vowed to give to Troylus and no one else? How dare he come at me thus while I slept? He has violated me!"

She looked at the child with horror.

"I don't want him. Take him away, take him away!"

She became so hysterical that her aunt feared she would do herself and the child an injury. As she was racking her brains for what to do, a great bird with the face of a handsome youth appeared at the window. Its feathers were of gold and burning red.

"Do not fear, good woman," said the bird-youth. "I will take care of the child for now. He will be nourished by goddesses in the immortal realm. And when the time is right, I will bring him back."

Comforted by the sight of the divine being, she placed the baby between the bird's wings, and it flew away until it was nothing more than a burning speck on the horizon.

When King Zelland heard that his daughter had awoken from her illness, he was overjoyed. He gave an extravagant party that lasted a whole week, at which numerous libations were poured out to the gods, particularly Mars and Venus.

But Zellandine remained pale and sad. She stayed in the tower room, tended by her aunt, and though she grew stronger in her body, her spirits sank lower.

One day towards the end of April, when birds were nesting and the hawthorn beginning to blossom, Zellandine was sitting in her tower window, looking out over the gardens. She thought of Troylus, and the time they had walked together in the maze, picking flowers and laughing. Suddenly, she noticed the ring on her finger. This was the ring she had given Troylus at their betrothal! The one she normally wore, the ring he had given her, was gone. There was only one person who could have made the switch.

"It was Troylus, Aunt," she said, holding up her hand and showing her the ring. "Troylus came to me that night. The gods must have assisted him, but it was he. We must send word to him to come as soon as possible. Oh, where is our son? How could I have sent him away?"

The aunt shook her head, doubtfully.

"Who knows where Troylus is now? It is best you put this incident behind you and let your father find you a new husband. No one will know you had a baby; it doesn't even show any more. And you're a young girl, with your whole life ahead of you. Why shouldn't you marry?"

The very idea of this filled Zellandine with horror.

"No, aunt! I will pray to Venus, that Troylus might be found and come back to me."

It was true that Troylus had gone far away. The magical bird-youth had flown him all the way to his home in Scotland, so he would not be late for his sister's wedding. After the festivities had died down, his first thought was to return to Zellandine. But the way was long, and he no longer had the magic bird with him, nor other men to accompany him. So, he must make the long journey on foot, on horseback and by water, encountering all the perils of weather, wild beasts and enemy warriors. At last, he reached the island of Zelland but – oh, horror! – the King had decided he would wed Zellandine to another knight called Neroen and was holding a tournament in his honour. Without a thought, Troylus entered the lists, although he kept his identity a secret, jousting with a blank shield. Love and jealously spurred him on, and he acquitted himself with as much honour as a knight may desire, especially against his rival suitor.

At the banquet after the tournament, Troylus found it hard to eat. He wanted to speak to Zellandine, but King Zelland was sitting across from her, and Neroen was sitting next to her. He took the nearest seat he could, and removed his hood, so everyone could see his face.

"Don't I know you?" said the King, scowling.

"Indeed, you do," said Troylus. "I am Troylus of Royalville, in Scotland."

He did not mention his former betrothal to Zellandine, but she glanced at his right hand. There on his smallest finger was a gold ring with an emerald at its centre, the very ring he had once given her. In response, she rested her own right hand against her cheek, so that Troylus could see the matching ring on her finger.

As soon as the dancing began, the pair slipped behind a pillar and began to talk, their words tumbling over one another. Troylus told Zellandine of his visit to her tower, she of the birth of their son and how the bird-youth had borne him away.

"They told me Mars had sired him on me," she said, "but I know it was you."

She wept, and Troylus cupped her cheek in his hand.

"My lovely friend, I am so sorry that I had to do what I did. It was the only way to wake you."

"It was the right way, for me," she said. "For that is what the Fates ordained at my birth. And now we have a son, if only we knew where he was."

She sighed, and Troylus held her close.

"Father has forgotten our betrothal entirely. He means to wed me to Neroen, unless you help me."

"Then run away with me, to the court of King Perceforest. I know he will protect us," said Troylus.

Zellandine agreed. She told no one but a maid, who helped pack her clothes and jewels. Troylus arranged for three horses to be saddled, one for him, one for Zellandine and one for the maid. They met as arranged in the stable-yard, and were just tightening the girths, when a spark of golden flame appeared in the sky. It grew larger and larger until, standing before them, was the magical bird-youth. And nestled in the golden feathers on his back was the baby son Zellandine had born to Troylus.

Both young parents wept at the sight of their child, and took him in their arms, one after the other.

"No need of horses when I am here," said the bird-youth. "Climb on my back and I will take you to King Perceforest's court, all three of you."

Zellandine and Troylus, with their baby son in their arms, climbed on the bird's back.

"Farewell," said Zellandine to the maid. Tell my father and aunt that Mars the god of war has come for me and is taking me away to his own country."

With that, the bird flexed his mighty wings and together they soared into the night sky, in a blaze of gold and burning red.

Pygmalion and Galatea

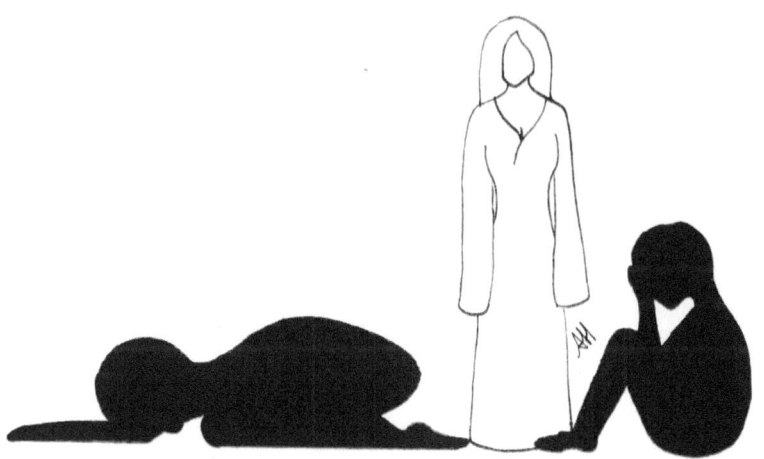

6

Pygmalion and Galatea

The story of 'Pygmalion and Galatea' comes from Greek mythology. Many people find it to be a misogynistic and deeply troubling story, but I have always seen it as an asexual tale, about longing for a Platonic Ideal of love and beauty in a sex-crazed world.

This re-imagining is partly inspired by Ovid's version in his epic poem *Metamorphoses* (c.AD 8) and partly by an episode from *Phantastes* (1858) by the Victorian writer of fairy tales, George MacDonald. In it, the protagonist Anodos discovers a marble cave, where he is reminded of Pygmalion, the Half-Marble Prince and Sleeping Beauty. He frees the form of a woman from the rock, but she flees from him. He spends the rest of the book pursuing her as his Ideal, while simultaneously trying to lose his Shadow.

Pygmalion the sculptor was sad. He longed to find a companion with whom to share his life, but when he looked around his homeland of Cyprus, it seemed that everyone was obsessed with only one thing. Sex.

Wherever he looked - at festivals, in poetry, in the marketplace - there was no escape from thrusting horns and gyrating hips. It seemed that the ultimate goal of everyone's life was to copulate as often and as raunchily as possible.

"Where is the beauty and romance in that?" he thought. "Why does anyone need sex, anyway? Love should be about coming into the secret garden, listening to the song of nightingales beneath the moon. Surely that is a much better kind of ecstasy? Am I the only person who dreams of a pure, chaste love? Does no one understand?"

And he remembered the words of the philosopher Plato, that Ideal forms exist before real, live creations.

"Perhaps my Ideal partner exists somewhere in the world of ideas, and I have only to dream her into being," he thought.

As the days went by, he spent more and more time daydreaming about his Ideal of Love and Beauty, but nothing seemed to change. Cyprus remained as sex-driven as ever, and Pygmalion met no one who shared his hopes and dreams.

One day, there was a festival to honour Venus, goddess of love. As Cyprus was the birthplace of Venus, it was ill fortune not to attend, but Pygmalion went with a heavy heart. Musicians and dancers filled the streets on the way to the temple. White heifers with gold on their horns processed to the altar to be slaughtered as offerings. Pygmalion shuffled through the crowd to place his own offering of flowers and incense at Venus' temple.

There, on the steps of the temple stood the Mirror of Venus: three huge discs of polished copper, joined by hinges and arranged in a concave arc. The left-hand mirror showed Venus in her Earthly aspect, as goddess of fertile Nature and all that grows and multiplies. The right-hand mirror showed her in Pygmalion's hated aspect of Venus Infernal, goddess of lust and vanity. But the central mirror showed the Heavenly Venus, the goddess of Divine Beauty and Love.

"Oh, Divine Venus," Pygmalion prayed, laying down his offering. "Grant that I might discover my Ideal partner and no longer be alone."

In his ears, Pygmalion heard the hush of the surf, and a voice whispering:

"Step inside my mirror, if you would gain your heart's desire."

Then it seemed to Pygmalion that the central mirror grew and grew, until it was no longer a disc of copper, but a portal. Pygmalion stepped through and found himself in a cave of white marble, lit from above by a rosy light. Birdsong and the soft laughter of a stream could be heard from the forest outside.

Pygmalion sat on a rock in the centre of the cave and looked around. Then he stood up and looked more closely. The faint outline of a woman's form was trapped within the marble.

"I must free her," said Pygmalion.

As if by magic, he found the tools of his trade were in his hand:

the sculptor's chisel and hammer. Delicately, he chipped at the rock, a fragment here, a shaving there. To rush would be to damage the lovely form. Already, Pygmalion could see she was exactly the sort of person he had imagined.

"I will call you Galatea," he said. "How I will love you!"

He kept working, oblivious to all else but the form taking shape in front of him. Her shoulders were now defined, the curve of her back, each toe of her feet. And her face! He had seen that sweet smile, those twinkling eyes night after night in his sleep, since he was a boy.

She was almost complete. Pygmalion stood back to view his work, wiping sweat and dust from his brow. At that moment, there was a crack, a grinding of rock on rock and - miracle of miracles - Galatea stepped down from the cavern wall, no longer a statue but a living woman. Here was Pygmalion's very Ideal of Love and Beauty come to life before him. Pale as marble she was and dressed in a flowing white robe. Her cheek and fingers were almost translucent, so the rosy light of the cave shone through her. Pygmalion gasped and rushed to embrace her.

"Galatea! My Galatea!" he cried.

The marble woman stepped back, scorn in her eyes.

"Who gave you permission to touch me?" she said.

And before Pygmalion could stop her, she ran out into the forest. He tried to follow but could see no sign of her. He had only managed to touch one shoulder with the tip of his fingers, and that was as cold as stone.

He sank back onto the rock, his head in his hands.

"What a heartless fool I am!" he said. "I prayed to Venus for a partner unlike the men and women of my island. A companion of the heart, not the flesh. And the moment I find her, what do I do but act just like them, rushing to speak with bodies instead of souls?"

He kicked away the sculptor's tools and got to his feet.

"Goddess of Divine Beauty and Love, I will not fail you again. I will seek out Galatea and make amends."

So saying, he left the cave and set off into the forest, the way he had seen Galatea flee. He was no woodsman and saw few signs of her passage save a broken branch and occasional footprint. The sun was hot overhead, and he found himself seeking deeper and deeper shade. Stumbling, he tripped over roots and ivy. The undergrowth rustled, a threat of wild beasts. If night were to fall while he was here, Pygmalion feared he would be lost forever.

Suddenly, the trees thinned out. Pygmalion found himself at the entrance to what he knew was a sacred grove. But this grove was not sacred to Venus, but to Diana, goddess of chastity. It was a place where men fear to tread, lest they be found unworthy as Actaeon was, who was transformed to a stag and hunted to death by his own hounds.

Pygmalion broke a branch from the golden bough, as must all who enter that place. With humble steps, he walked to the centre of the grove. There, beneath the shade of a cypress, stood Galatea, a statue once more. When Pygmalion saw her, he fell at her feet and wet the ground with his tears.

"Galatea, forgive me," he said. "Or not Galatea, if that's not what you wish to be called. I saw a face like yours in my dreams and believe that Venus led me to free you from the marble cave. Yet I would never possess you. I wish to be your friend and companion. I will not even attempt to hold your hand unless you tell me so."

At this, he swallowed hard, for he did wish to hold her hand, to rest his head against hers, to hug warmly. But he wished still more to explore the unknown contours of her soul, and that she might explore his.

It was many minutes before Pygmalion found the courage to raise his eyes. When he did, he saw Galatea a woman once more, no longer white as marble but fully flesh and blood.

"I dreamt of you when I was marble," she said. "All through the long ages of rock and stone, I waited for a friend like you, not bound by the obsession of this island. And now you have come and proved yourself true. Let us walk together, Pygmalion, and be companions always."

Slowly, they turned away from the grove and walked back through the forest. Strange to tell, it wasn't long before they found themselves on the road to Pygmalion's village, arriving just as the moon first arose in the evening sky. Galatea reached out and took Pygmalion's hand. And it was warm.

The Ivory Maid

7

The Ivory Maid

'The Ivory Maid' can be read as a gender-reversed *Pygmalion*, in which it is the maiden herself who has created her Ideal of Love and Beauty.

It is one of my early stories, written as part of a collection, *My True Love Sent to Me* (2009), where it appeared as 'Twelve Lords A-Leaping'. It was inspired by the medieval romances of Chrétien de Troyes (c.1170–82) and the Breton lais of Marie de France (fl.late twelfth century).

A t one time in the kingdom of Logres, birthplace of many noble knights, there dwelt a knight whose name was Girflet. He was both courteous and liberal (as a knight should be) but he was also sad and lonely, for there was no lady to whom he had given his heart and whose token he could wear when he went abroad.

It happened one day that Girflet had been badly wounded in a tournament. As he rode home, his wound became so painful that he needed to stop and rest. He had been riding close to a river, so he left his squire and his horse and began to remove his armour in order to bathe his wounded leg, hoping to ease the pain. As he began to wash, he saw a marvellous thing. A ship was sailing towards him. Its pure white sails were made of silk, and its ropes glinted as if spun with silver. At its prow was the figure of an ivory woman, exquisitely beautiful, with two whole sapphires for her eyes.

A noble knight in those times never refused an adventure, and so, filled with wonder, Girflet climbed aboard the ship. There was no one on the deck, which shone as if no foot had ever trod there. Girflet could hear nothing but the gentle lapping of the water and a slight creak of timbers. Going below, he was amazed to find a bed, laid with the most expensive covers, all in various hues of white, cream and ivory, with white lace curtains hanging from the posts. The top coverlet was embroidered all over with delicate cobwebs and snowflakes of the finest silver thread. Girflet was afraid to stay there, lest the blood from his wound should spoil the bed's perfect whiteness, but seemingly against his will, a great weariness overcame him, and he dropped down, laying his head upon the lacy pillow.

When he woke, he found the ship had carried him to a place he had never seen before. Great willow trees bent down to embrace the water on each side, and the prow of the ship cut a path through hundreds of white lilies. By the bank of the river stood a palace, the like of which Girflet had scarcely imagined in his dreams. Its walls were made of the purest, smoothest marble and seemed to shine in the rays of the sun. Many tall turrets pointed to the heavens, and the breeze caught banners embroidered with the same cobweb and snowflake emblems that had covered him while he slept. He rubbed his eyes, but the palace remained.

Stepping ashore, he went towards the palace, expecting at any moment to be met by some servant or other, perhaps a guard or a labourer working the surrounding fields, but none appeared. Instead, the mighty gates swung open for him, and he went inside alone. Instantly, he jumped with surprise at the sight of a whole host of knights apparently standing guard all along the walls. But a moment's thought told him this was just an illusion. The walls were in fact made entirely of mirrors from floor to ceiling, so all he could see as he went along was his own image, constantly repeated and reflected. Girflet was deeply intrigued and began to explore the baffling palace, hoping to find its master.

Soon he came to a large central chamber in the shape of a dodecagon, the walls of which were panelled with twelve huge and magnificent mirrors, expertly gilded with silver. The floor was ebony, with a great silver cobweb traced into it; a line from the centre extended to the centre of each mirror. The whole chamber was lit by a pale and changeable light, yet there was not a single window to be found. Looking around, Girflet suddenly gasped with horror. The reflections in these mirrors were not his own, but rather, of twelve handsome young lords, each one more handsome than the last. They were all dressed in tunics of black with silver snowflakes at their hearts, and their melting eyes were filled with sorrow.

"Who are you?" Girflet said.

He hardly expected them to reply, yet the words left his mouth and echoed round the eerie chamber.

"We are the prisoners of the Ivory Maid," the youngest and most handsome lord said, his voice seeming to come from the depths of the earth. "One by one, she enticed and entrapped us. Now we are slaves in her chamber of mirrors. Every night she stands at the centre of the cobweb and gazes at us for hours at a time. We know neither warmth, nor touch, nor conversation. All is cold within the gaze of her sapphire eyes."

"Is there no way you can be freed?" Girflet said.

"There is but one way," the second most handsome lord replied, his eyes as grey as the stormy sea. "This ebony chamber has never seen the sun. It is lit only by the magical light of its snowflake ceiling. Were the sun to shine on us, then these mirrors would break, and we should be free. For they cannot be broken by any other means, neither by fists, nor by stones, nor by the weight of a battle axe."

Girflet pondered this for a while. He did not see how he - alone, wounded and weaponless - could break through a roof of solid marble to let in the sun. But he could not bear to think that such noble lords of men should be kept prisoner in this manner, never to know the warmth of love or fellowship. So he said, "I am at your service, my lords. I will do what I can."

And he left the chamber to find a way to the roof.

The palace was large and extremely puzzling. Girflet wandered through corridors, up and down staircases, in and out of rooms of various dimensions, baffled and confused by the constant reflections. He was tired and a little sick. His leg ached. He began to wonder if the Ivory Maid really existed, as there was no sign of her or indeed of any life at all in the palace. All was silent, and he saw no one but himself.

At last, when he was on the verge of giving up hope, he came to a winding staircase leading out onto marble battlements and began, precariously, to cross the roof of the palace. The sun was at its full height, and he could hear the singing of birds in the trees below him. He blinked several times to try to cope with the light after the dim paleness of the palace corridors, but the sun, the height and the earlier loss of blood made him dizzy. Despite being a knight of Logres, he was forced to sit down in the nearest available space. Suddenly, his bandaged wound burst open again. The blood seeped through his clothes and dripped onto the marble rooftop, a dark pool of red against the spotless white. As Girflet watched helplessly, his warm blood began to sink into the marble, melting its coldness. Deeper and deeper it went, until the first single drop of blood fell to the ebony floor of the chamber of mirrors, right in the centre of the silver web.

At that moment, the rays of the sun shone through the tiny hole in the ceiling and glanced off one mirror after another. With a resounding crash, the glass shattered, and the twelve young lords leapt free of their prisons. Laughing and clasping one another's hands in the sunlight, they shouted their thanks to Girflet, each promising to reward him with great treasure when they reached home. Then they ran through the mirrored corridors and into the free air where swift horses awaited them.

Girflet listened to their footsteps and youthful shouts echoing away. Then he slowly crossed the roof and came down the stairs, dragging his wounded leg behind him. As he did so, he heard the faint sound of a woman weeping. He followed the sound and found that it came from a tiny room at the top of a turret. Gently opening the door, Girflet saw a maiden dressed from head to foot in purest white, with a silver belt and a veil of lace covering her long hair. She was seated by the window, and tears spilled from her clear blue eyes, rolling down her cheeks and dripping onto her skirts as she turned and looked towards Girflet.

"Alas, what have you done to me, sir knight?" she said. "The beauty of my house is overthrown. My mirrors are broken, and my lords are now fled, whose like I shall never see again as long as I live."

And she wept again. Girflet thought her exceedingly beautiful, more beautiful than any lady he had ever seen in his life. In his heart he pitied her, in spite of what she had done, because she was so young and so sad. Although he knew nothing of the arts of love, he longed to see her smile and to fill her palace with warmth, where yet there had been only coldness. So he said, "Though I am neither as young nor as handsome as they were, and though I am a knight only and not a lord, yet I will stay a while and help rebuild your house for you, to make amends for what I have done."

He knelt before her and held out his hand. And the tears of the Ivory Maid dropped onto his hand and his knee, glistening like silver.

And at that moment, his wound was healed.

Companions of the Grail

8

Companions of the Grail

This short episode from the Arthurian legend comes from 'The Tale of the Sankgreal' in Sir Thomas Malory's epic *Le Morte D'Arthur* (1485). Unlike his Victorian incarnation, Malory's Sir Galahad is a very human character, who seems embarrassed by his fame as "the best knight of the world" and longs for a closer relationship with his father, Sir Lancelot.

'Companions of the Grail' tells of the convening of the fellowship of four that will achieve the quest of the Holy Grail. To me, Sir Galahad comes across as asexual, as does Sir Perceval's sister. (Malory doesn't give her a name, so I have decided to call her Pearl). During the quest, the two develop what could be read as a chaste romance. By contrast, Perceval is a virgin who has taken a vow of chastity, while Bors has given up sex for the quest. Thus, in a brief tale, the difference between asexuality, virginity and chastity is perfectly illustrated.

A magical ship was sailing along the coast. In it lay the knight Sir Perceval, fast asleep. Truth to tell, he was more sorrowful than weary. He was on the quest of the Holy Grail and had made a vow of chastity, but a recent test had brought him so close to breaking his vow that he was ashamed of himself. So, he had laid him down to sleep and the ship had sailed on without his knowledge. And now it was about to stop for another knight.

Sir Bors had been hastening to the coast following a vision. When he saw the ship, he stepped aboard and saw Sir Perceval lying there.

"Just the man I was looking for," he said, and shook Perceval awake.

"Go away, I'm sulking," said Sir Perceval. "And who are you anyway?"

Sir Bors smiled and took off his helmet.

"Bors!" cried Perceval and slapped him on the back.

They were soon chatting away and catching up on adventures.

"At least you passed the chastity test." Perceval sighed.

"Perce, I nearly killed my own brother. I'm hardly a success," said Bors. "Anyway, you're still a virgin, aren't you? Believe me, there are things in my past that I'm not proud of."

They looked out at the horizon.

"All we need now is our friend, Sir Galahad," said Perceval. He thought a while. "I bet he wouldn't fail the chastity test."

"I don't think it would be a test for him," said Bors. "He's not made that way."

Meanwhile, Sir Galahad was resting at a hermitage on his way to the castle of King Pelles, his grandfather. It was because of Pelles' troubles that the Knights of Camelot were seeking the Holy Grail. He had a wound that would not heal, and all his lands lay waste. Only the Grail could bring restoration.

In the middle of the night, someone knocked on the door. Galahad went to answer it and found a lady standing there.

"I've been sent to escort you to your next adventure," she said. "Come with me."

So, right there and then, in the middle of the night, Sir Galahad and the lady mounted their horses and rode away. And where should the lady bring Sir Galahad but to the magical ship carrying his two friends, Bors and Perceval.

That was a merry meeting! The three brother-knights laughed long and loud, shaking hands and clapping each other on the back.

"But who is our new companion?" said Sir Perceval.

"Don't you recognise me?" said the lady. "We haven't met since we were children, but I'm your sister, Pearl."

"Sister!" cried Perceval and hugged her tight. "Now our fellowship is really complete."

But soon the four companions had a challenge on their hands. There were some narrow rocks ahead, and their ship couldn't pass through. It looked like they would be stuck, until they spotted a second ship waiting at the other side. Together, they clambered across the rocks and into the new ship. They could already see that it was even more magical than the first. The very ropes shimmered with enchantment. In the middle of the ship was a magnificent bed with a canopy of silk. At the foot of the bed lay a sword, partly drawn out of its sheath.

It was a wondrous thing. The pommel was a precious stone of many colours that changed in the light. The hilt was inlaid with the ribs of two marvellous beasts: the Serpent of Caledonia, whose virtue is that no one who handles him shall be weary or hurt, and the Fish of the Euphrates, whose virtue is that the one who handles him shall think on neither joys nor sorrows, but only on the task at hand.

On the sheath of the sword were the words:

Only the greatest of all knights can wield me. If he bears me well, he will never be shamed. But if the wrong person tries to use me, I will be a cursed sword to him and fail him in his hour of greatest need.

Both Perceval and Bors tried to draw the sword, but they could not. Everyone looked at Galahad.

"I think we should just leave it alone." He shuffled his feet. "I know you all think I'm the greatest knight of the world, but what if I'm not? It's just asking for trouble."

Pearl laid a hand on Galahad's arm.

"Galahad, this is your sword. I know its history and the history of this ship. The ship first came to our land in the days of King Labor, your great-grandfather. At the time, there was war between him and King Hurlaine. During battle, Hurlaine was forced to flee, and he found this ship and this sword. He took the sword into battle and smote King Labor so hard upon the helm that he dropped dead in an instant.

"That was when the pestilence first came upon the land, turning it to a Waste Land, because of that Dolorous Stroke. King Hurlaine staggered back to the ship with the sword, then he, too, lay down and died. Since then, the sword has brought nothing but bad luck to anyone who tries to use it.

"A knight called Nacien once found the sword in the ship and praised its beauty. But when he tried to use it to defend himself, it shattered to pieces. He reforged the sword and returned it to its scabbard, but as soon as he left the ship, he was pierced in the foot, for he had never been worthy to draw it."

Galahad looked at Pearl, wide-eyed.

"Madam, you're so...knowledgeable."

Pearl only smiled and went on.

"Then, finally, your grandfather King Pelles came along, and tried to draw the sword that had maimed his father and cursed his lands. But he was pierced through both thighs with a spear for his attempt, and that wound has never healed, as you know.

"But now you are here, Sir Galahad. The quest of the Grail is your destiny, I know it is. That's why I've spent the last year making you a new sword-belt, to wear with this sword."

She opened her pack and took out a box. In it was a beautiful sword-belt, decorated with gold thread and precious stones, with a rich buckle of gold.

"I stitched my own hair into it," she said, blushing. "As soon as I knew this adventure was my destiny, I cut my off hair like a nun. I don't need it any more, for I'll never be a court lady again, nor be any man's wife."

"You might not need your hair, but I don't know where we'd be without you," said Sir Bors. "Isn't that right, Galahad?"

Galahad blushed.

"Let me gird the sword on you, Sir Galahad," said Pearl.

She girded the sword about his middle, while Galahad gripped the hilt.

Pearl sat back and looked Sir Galahad in the eye.

"Now I count myself the most blessed of maidens, to have armed the greatest knight of the world."

Sir Galahad's voice was gentle.

"Madam, I shall be your knight all the days of my life."

"Pearl's like Galahad, isn't she?" said Perceval, as the ship set sail. Galahad and Pearl were holding hands in the bow of the ship.

"Yes," said Bors. "I think she is. Which is just as well," he said after a while, "as I don't think either of them will outlive this quest."

And in his mind's eye, he saw a white city, and Pearl floating into it on this ship, dead but beautiful. And he saw Galahad reaching for the Grail and walking out of this world entirely, his body collapsing, useless, to the ground. And he saw a tomb wherein they both lay, together for eternity.

"But we'll help them achieve it, Perce," said Bors. "We won't fail."

"No," said Perceval. "We won't."

The ship sailed on.

82

Pearls and Roses

9

Pearls and Roses

The Virgin Mary has long been an important asexual icon to me. 'Pearls and Roses' is part of a family of fairy tales that includes 'Our Lady's Child' (Grimm) and 'The Lassie and her Godmother' (Asbjørnsen & Moe). These tales tell of a girl who goes to live with her godmother, the Virgin Mary, and opens a forbidden door, a motif also familiar from 'Bluebeard', although here the door reveals something heavenly rather than hellish. 'Pearls and Roses', however, takes a very different turn from its sister stories. Instead of marrying a prince, our heroine Maria is "indifferent to the stirrings of love". What I particularly like about this tale is the idea of asexuality being a "gift" given to the protagonist at birth. Armed with the knowledge that her identity is a positive thing, Maria can go on to create an alternative community based upon friendship and support.

'Pearls and Roses' comes from *The Turnip Princess: And Other Newly Discovered Fairy Tales* (2015), a book of tales collected by Franz Xaver von Schönwerth, a contemporary of the Brothers Grimm. The tales were collected in the 1850s but thought lost until 2009. The English translation is by Maria Tatar, where this story appears as 'Pearl Tears'.

There was once a knight who fell in love with his serving maid and married her. Can you imagine the scandal it caused? None of the local aristocracy attended the wedding. The husband's brother-knights refused to speak to him, and none of the high-born ladies would receive the wife. The couple were left alone in their castle, forgotten by their friends and rejected by their family.

But what did they care? They were in love. True, the Great Hall echoed somewhat emptily without any guests, and half the chambers were shut up, but they had each other. They drew the curtains about their bed, and lay all winter, wrapped in furs.

But New Year brought a new arrival. As blossom returned to the garden, the wife found she was with child. For the first time, the couple felt their isolation. Who would attend the birth? Who would be godparent when the child was christened? The nearer drew the time, the more anxious the parents became.

At last, the wife said to the husband:

"The child is coming soon, and it must have a godparent. Go out and ask the first person you see, be it lord, merchant, nun or beggar."

So, the husband went out to seek a godparent. He had scarcely left his own garden when he met an elegant lady in a veil of midnight blue.

"Of course, I will be your child's godmother," she said when the knight asked. "That is why I have come." And when the knight looked confused, she said: "Do you not recognise me? I am the Virgin Mary. I will take care of your child. Now hurry, your wife's time is near."

The knight could hardly refuse the Madonna, so he escorted her into the castle, where she assisted at the birth and brought comfort to the mother. The child was a girl. At her christening, she was given the name Maria, in honour of her noble godparent.

After the christening, the Madonna made ready to leave.

"I must go now," she said, "but I will come again, if ever Maria needs me. As for my christening gift to her, it is not of a kind you can perceive now, but it will become apparent as time goes by."

Years passed. Maria grew into a lively and curious child. But when she reached the age of seven, tragedy visited the castle. Maria's mother died. Both father and daughter mourned the kindly woman who had meant so much to them. But the knight knew it was impossible for him to bring up a girl-child without a wife. In his youth, he had married for love, but now he needed the support of his neighbours. So, he married a respectable woman of his own class, hoping she would raise his daughter to be a lady.

But the new stepmother did not take to Maria. There was something not right about the child, she thought. One day she would play at being a princess, the next at being a knight. And she would play with the stable boy or the goose girl just as happily as with the well-bred daughters of her new relatives. It was her ill breeding, the stepmother decided, the legacy of that jumped-up serving wench, her mother.

She began to treat Maria with contempt, then with spite. She would call her names, criticise her speech, her features, her way of walking. She cast Maria's toys on the ash heap and banished her favourite cat to the barn. And increasingly, she would give Maria menial chores that should have been the work of servants.

Maria became more and more unhappy. Her father the knight was troubled too, but he had promised to leave the raising of his daughter to his new wife. Perhaps this harsh treatment was for her own good?

But Maria only saw that she was hated and couldn't understand why. One day, she was so miserable that she curled up in a corner and cried until her clothes were drenched with tears.

Suddenly, a beautiful lady in a blue veil appeared.

"My dear child," said the Madonna, "I am your godmother. I made a vow to your mother that, if ever you were in need, I would come to you. Now, come." And she held out her hand. "I will take you to live with me."

Maria took the Virgin's hand, and together they walked deep into the woods. On the other side of a glade stood a mountain. Its sides were sheer and glittered like quartz. The Madonna knocked three times on the mountainside and, to Maria's astonishment, the outline of a door appeared. Noiselessly, it swung open, and the two went inside.

Within the mountain was a hidden palace. The Madonna led Maria through twelve different rooms. Each had strands and strands of pearls hanging from the walls. The floors and ceilings were mother-of-pearl, and the walls of rose marble. On every table and windowsill stood a bowl of roses, filled with crystal water.

"Maria, your job will be to tend my roses," the Madonna said. "You must water them every day and make sure they do not wilt. Can you do that?"

"Yes, godmother," said Maria.

"Very good." The Virgin stroked Maria's cheek. "Then we shall be very happy. Let us eat."

They sat down at a polished table, and plates of food floated out of nowhere, carried by invisible hands. Floating jugs poured wine and milk, and when Maria and the Madonna had had their fill, invisible hands cleared the table.

After dinner, the Madonna led Maria to a little bed in an alcove, covered by a starry canopy. She tucked her in and sang her lullabies, and Maria drifted off to sleep, happier than she had been in months.

So began Maria's life in the hidden palace. Every day, Maria and her godmother ate together, waited on by the same invisible hands. Every night, they read and sang together, before Maria slept in the starry bed. And every day, Maria tended the roses. There was something about this work that was just right for her, she thought. It answered a need deep inside her, though she knew not what it was.

One day, when Maria had reached the age of fifteen, the Madonna said, "I am going on a journey. I won't be gone long, and I'm sure I can trust you to look after the palace while I'm away."

"You can, you can, godmother," said Maria, eager for this chance to prove herself.

"In that case, I will give you the key to every chamber in the palace. You can go anywhere you like, only do not use this thirteenth key. The door it opens is forbidden."

"I won't, godmother," said Maria. "I'll do everything you say, and I'll water the roses every day."

"Good girl," said the Virgin. "I'll be back soon."

Maria was very excited by her new responsibility. She glided from room to room, trying to mimic the posture of the Virgin. She sat in the Madonna's chair and ordered food from the invisible servants. But by the third day, she grew bored. She peered out of the windows, trying to see beyond the starry blackness on the other side. In one window she saw a comet, in another a falling star. But she had seen such things before, and soon she was fingering the bunch of keys. What could the thirteenth key possibly open? She didn't even know the palace had thirteen doors.

Before long, she was going around the palace, feeling for hidden doors. And not long after that, behind a silver-threaded tapestry, she discovered an arch-shaped door with a sun and moon worked upon it in gold.

It was unlike anything else in the palace. Thrilled, Maria tried the thirteenth key in the lock. It turned easily. She opened the door and stepped inside.

She was standing in an enormous library. Polished shelves with rails of brass ran from floor to ceiling. They held more books than Maria had seen in her life, more than she knew existed. There were huge volumes held in place by chains, beautifully illustrated manuscripts embossed with gold leaf. There were scrolls, clay tablets, and records written in every script, from Sanskrit to Aztec to Norse Runes.

Sitting at a desk in the centre of the room, two figures were writing. One was a dazzling white like winter sunlight on snow: white clothes, white head, white hair. A gold sash was tied across his chest, and his feet beneath the desk seemed to glow like bronze in a furnace. The second figure was wreathed in mist, as if Maria saw him on top of a mountain. Through the mist, he gleamed as if made of jasper and carnelian; a rainbow surrounded his head.

At the sound of the opening door, the white figure looked up sharply. He fixed Maria with his gaze, which now seemed to be of fire, white-hot. She tried to look away but could not. The fire blazed hotter and hotter, piercing her very soul.

When the Madonna returned home, she found Maria slumped in front of the secret door, the keys scattered across the pearly floor, her eyes unseeing.

The Virgin shook her to wakefulness and revived her with a drink. Then she turned sad eyes upon Maria.

"Oh, Maria! Why did you disobey? What you saw was the Lord Almighty and his Son, writing out the destinies of all mankind, and endowing them with gifts with which to live their lives. Had you stayed with me longer, you might have come to understand your own gift, but none may look upon the destinies of others. That is not for you to know.

"Now I am afraid you must leave me and return to the world. I am sorry to lose you, but I hope we will meet again one day."

The Madonna gave Maria a white gown and a crown of roses to wear and pointed her in the direction of her father's castle. Maria found her way through the woods easily, though she walked with a heavy heart. She wondered what she would find when she returned home.

When she reached the castle, she found the stonework crumbling and the moat filled with weeds. Inside, the walls were bare of hangings and the swords above the fireplace were gone. While Maria had been away, her father had fallen upon hard times. Her stepmother had borne him two sons but had been far too extravagant with his wealth. As a result, he had lost all his fortune.

When the knight saw Maria, he was overjoyed. He thought she must have died long ago. The little boys were awestruck by the pretty girl in the white gown, who walked so silently. But the stepmother was incensed by Maria's return.

"Another mouth to feed?" she said to the knight. "Taking bread from the mouths of your heirs! Well, if she must stay, she must earn her keep. She's old enough."

The stepmother stripped Maria of her new gown, to sell it, and gave her an old, grey smock instead. She sent Maria to the kitchen, where she was forced to do the most menial tasks without pay, and to make her bed in a niche by the stove.

Now she was degraded and dirty, Maria's step-brothers no longer stood in awe of her. They taunted her and called her a ragamuffin. One day, they took to throwing stones at her. They pelted her so hard that she began to bleed. She retreated to the kitchen and bent over a basin to wash off the blood, weeping hard. Drops of blood fell into the water, and each tear hit the bottom of the bowl with a chinking sound.

The stepmother came into the kitchen to scold the children for their constant bickering. She snatched the bowl from Maria's hand. As she did so, she noticed something shiny in the bottom of the basin. Maria's tears had become pearls.

The stepmother was delighted. With money raised from selling the pearls, the family could return to its former lifestyle. They held a grand ball, to which even Maria was invited. When she heard the news, Maria laughed for joy. As she laughed, roses tumbled from her mouth. She twisted them into a wreath and wore it in her hair at the ball.

Maria loved the ball. It was the first time in her life she had been present at such an occasion. She had never heard such music, tasted such food or seen so many people dressed in such fine clothes. She danced the galliard, the pavanne, the allemande and the sarabande. Her beauty dazzled the guests, and many young men begged a dance of her. There was something in their eyes Maria could not understand. Yet she enjoyed their company, laughing and joking with them and with the young women until it was almost dawn.

But the good times could not last. As before, the stepmother was incautious with money. The funds from the pearls ran out. Again, Maria was banished to the kitchen. Again, the step-brothers taunted her and threw stones. Again, Maria wept into the washbasin. And with each tear, a pearl would chink into the bottom of the bowl.

Once more, the stepmother was delighted with the outcome. Once more, she sold the pearls and spent the money on a grand ball. Once more, Maria laughed roses, and danced with young knights and barons.

One young baron in particular asked her to dance again and again. When the time came for refreshments, he tried to take her out onto the ramparts, as he said he had something particular to ask her. But this only made Maria anxious and confused. She steered the young baron back into the hall, back to the laughter and tall tales.

Yet again, the stepmother wasted the family fortune. This time, she was convinced it was Maria's fault.

"You could have wed a baron! I saw the way he looked at you. You could have helped this family instead of being a constant drain on your poor father."

"But I didn't want to," Maria said. "When I dance with men, I feel nothing."

"What have feelings to do with it?" the stepmother muttered, and slapped Maria hard across the face.

As the weeks went by, Maria's brothers and stepmother tormented and persecuted Maria. She wept often, although she knew her tears simply made more pearls for her stepmother to waste.

One day, an old servant said to her:

"This cannot go on. I've served this family all my life, but I won't stand for it any more, the way that woman treats you. Next time you weep, give the bowl to me. I'm not afraid of that hag; what have I got to lose at my age? We'll fill a bowl and leave this place together."

The old woman's words gave Maria courage. When the bowl was full, they left the castle together at dead of night. They travelled to a distant town, where they used the pearls to buy a modest house. For a time, they were happy, and the house was filled with roses.

But Maria's beauty meant that young men would not leave her alone. Wealthy merchants and bankers, students at the university, even the son of the Lord Mayor came to ask for her hand. Maria felt nothing for any of them. Even the idea of marriage was one she could not comprehend. But what was she to do? Her aged companion would not be with her forever. Was she to spend all her life weeping tears of pearl, just so that she might live?

"Mother Mary, give me wisdom!" she prayed.

In an instant, the Madonna stood before her, veiled in blue just as Maria remembered her from childhood. She touched Maria's head in blessing. Then she smiled:

"My dear child! There's no need to worry. You have discovered the gift I gave you in the cradle: the gift of being indifferent to the stirrings of love. Now that you know it for yourself, you are ready to take up your destiny. Come with me."

Maria – with the old servant following behind – went with the Virgin to the side of the glittering mountain. The Virgin knocked three times and the door to the palace opened. It was all exactly as Maria remembered it.

"I am moving on from this region," the Madonna said. "I have other people to help and other tasks to complete. I leave this palace to you. All of it, even the key to the thirteenth room." She smiled. "For you are now mature enough to know what to do with it. Here, you can shelter all who are ill and impoverished. And this" – she stooped to bless the old woman – "shall be your very first guest."

So, Maria moved into the palace inside the mountain, along with her companion. There she provided shelter and sustenance for all who were in need. The twelve rooms were filled with love and friendship. And somehow, those who most needed help would turn up in the forest, right where Maria could emerge and take them into the mountain. If ever she needed advice, Maria would knock on the door of the thirteenth room and the Father and Son would advise her. But never again did she try to peep at their library. She knew the destinies of others were none of her business.

All her friends said Maria was a good and godly woman. She lived a long life. When she died, they laid her out in a white gown with a crown of red roses in her hair. And some swore that – for one moment – a perfumed breeze blew past and Maria was young and beautiful once more. The Virgin Mary had come to take her home.

The Ice Queen and
the Mer-King

10

The Ice Queen and the Mer-King

I wrote 'The Ice Queen and the Mer-King' at a time when I was struggling to understand my identity and put it into words. The language of fairy tale seemed the most natural to use. I have always been drawn to "women in towers" stories. The tower can represent so many things: inviolate self-protection, social anxiety, frustration, lack of choice. As a teenager, I felt a great affinity with the heroine of Alfred, Lord Tennyson's 'The Lady of Shalott' (1833). The Lady of the poem is unable to leave her tower, engaging with the outside world only through a magic mirror. When she feels the stirrings of unrequited love for Sir Lancelot and dares to look at him directly, a curse comes upon her and she dies.

Another poem I have always found to be deeply moving is Matthew Arnold's 'The Forsaken Merman' (1849), inspired by the Scandinavian folk tale 'Agneta and the Sea King'. The merman is represented as a tragic, romantic hero, mourning the desertion of his human wife who, "left lonely for ever the kings of the sea". This tale combines imagery from both. It first appeared in *New Fairy Tales* in February 2009.

There was once, so the story goes, a King who subdued the surrounding nations with the might of his sword, and all feared him. And when he had conquered the nations to the west and the south, he made war on the icemen who ruled the frozen wasteland to the north, beyond the mountains. Then there was battle on the plains of ice for many days, but the soldiers of the Warrior King outnumbered the icemen with their sparkling javelins, and the plains fell. For a prize of war, the king from the south demanded the elder daughter of the ice prince for his wife. He carried her away captive to his home among the heathlands and the rushing rivers and made her his Queen.

Never in all his days had the King seen such a rare beauty as the ice princess from the frozen waste. Her skin shone and glittered in the sun. Some say the sun shone right through it, leaving rainbows in every room through which she passed. Her eyes were as blue as the clear sky on a January morning, and each delicate strand of her flowing hair was made from a single icicle.

Too rare and too delicate was the new Queen for the palace of the King within his fortified city. He could not regale her in the mighty feast hall of his fathers, where the trophies of war hung above the great fireplace and unspeakable desires burned in the eyes of his warriors and chieftains. He could not promenade her in the scented gardens where the daughters of the ancient houses whispered by the trellises and the jealous sun winked maliciously from behind the clouds.

So, the King took his Queen of ice and locked her in the upper room of a tower. It stood on an island in a coastal bay, where the great river flowing from the mountains met the dark and changeable sea. Here she remained, looking out from her window at night, as the waves crashed and tumbled, singing a lament in the cold chiming tongue of her people. Her breath as she sang was like clouds of snowflakes falling in a mist. It fell slowly to meet the restless surface of the sea, each flake for one moment a glistening star before it was gone forever.

Each week, the King would unlock the door of the Queen's chamber with an iron key and bring her down to the room beneath her own, a cold room with gloomy tapestries and a panelled bed. There he would embrace her roughly and, with each embrace, one icicle strand of the Queen's hair would break off and fall to the ground with a crash. When the King was gone, the Queen, returning to her chamber, would weep and mourn the breaking of her delicate hair, shedding hailstone tears. These too would fall into the night, and the wind would carry them away into the heart of the sea.

Now, beneath the waves that roared about the island, lay the kingdom of the merfolk. For long centuries beyond the accounting of men, they had ruled the ocean depths. But unlike the King above the surface were they, because they ruled with equity and not by the sword.

Although their King wielded the trident, and the power of the waves was at his command, he used it but seldom. He took counsel among the lords of the merfolk and understood the ways of the many creatures that swim the unseen depths. And the pulse of the ocean was the beating of his own heart.

So, it happened that, as the merfolk feasted at night upon thrones of pearl and shared the fellowship cup together in their coral gardens, they looked far above them and saw the glittering of stars. It seemed to them that there were constellations in the heavens. Each star gleamed for one moment and then went dark as another appeared, as unlike the first as it was unlike the next. Magical and mysterious to the lords of the sea were the stars that were the breath of the Ice Queen. It happened also that, as they swam in clear lagoons beyond the knowledge of mariners, pearls fell softly through the sea towards them, no bigger than the scales of the tiniest fish. But when they tried to touch the pearls that were the Ice Queen's tears, they melted in their hands.

And the King of the merfolk declared that they should all swim up to the surface to see what these marvels were, that came to them from the world of air. So, they rose together at night upon the back of a wave, singing their haunting songs. There, in the window of the tower, they saw the Ice Queen with her clear blue eyes, weeping into the night.

The Queen looked through her tears and beheld the merfolk riding the waves and their hair blowing about them in the windy night. She lifted up her voice and sang mournfully in the chiming tongue she had learned beyond the mountains. Then the merfolk were glad, for they saw again those stars beneath the stars that had glittered on the surface of the sea. But the deep green eyes of their King were thoughtful and sad. Long into the night, the Ice Queen and the merfolk sang together in a strange and mysterious harmony. At last, as the first light of day showed pale upon the mountain tops, the merfolk turned and dived into the sea with a splashing of their powerful tails.

From that night onwards, the lords of the sea would rise often from their thrones to sing with the Ice Queen. All along the rocks they would sit, the jewels of the ocean gleaming wet on their blue-green breasts. And, from high in the window, the snowflakes of the Ice Queen's breath would flutter around their heads. All the while, the deep green eyes of the Mer-King were fixed on the lonely Ice Queen, with her rainbow-white skin and her beautiful broken hair. So, it came to be that the King of the Sea conceived in his heart a love for the Queen in the tower. And she, looking down at his noble face, wise with the changeable mysteries of the sea, also felt the pangs of love, for the very first time.

At that time, their love was a secret, locked deep in the heart of each. The silence between them could not be broken, for the language of the Ice Queen was as strange to the merfolk as theirs was to her. But, as one night gave way to another, so they gradually came to understand one another, and to speak, as well as to sing, together. The Ice Queen told the merpeople of her home in the frozen north; of the glittering palaces of crystal with many turrets, and the sleighs drawn by white reindeer that once carried her through frozen forests of silver glass. She told of the battles with the King from the south and of how he had carried her away, far from her home and all she loved. And the tiny pearls of her hailstone tears rained into the ocean. The Mer-King told her of the gardens beneath the sea where fish of a thousand colours swim through endless grasses. He told of the hearts of those who rule the sea, which are gentle and loving toward the tiniest creature that floats there. And, beneath the moon and the stars, their talk became ever more tender.

Now the Queen dreaded more than ever the turning of the iron key, and she wept more bitterly at the roughness that broke the icicle strands of her hair. Each time the King summoned her downstairs, she feared that he would see the heart of the ocean beginning to creep into her blue eyes. All that consoled her was the coming of the night and the pounding of the waves. Then one day, when she felt she could endure no more, the King did not appear at his appointed hour. Instead, the squire who held his horse came to tell her that the King had fallen in battle to the warlike Princes of the Scattered Isles and would visit her no more. Then the iron lock was broken, and the Queen walked for the first time on the grass and rocks of the island and sang a song of freedom that swirled in frosty clouds about her. The song of the Ice Queen pierced the sea and came to the ears of those who sat on thrones of pearl.

That night, the Mer-King rose from his ocean kingdom alone, and his wave lashed at the rock like thunder. In his hand, he held a necklace of coral with a jewel that glowed with every colour under the sea. He held it out to the Ice Queen with words of love, and humbly begged that she would come back with him to the kingdom of the merfolk and sit beside him forever.

Now the heart of the Ice Queen was filled with pain. She said to the Mer-King:

"I love you more than all the crystals of the silver forest. But in your kingdom, I should dissolve away to nothingness. Where you swim, I cannot follow, except in my heart."

And though the salt of the ocean came to the Mer-King's eyes, he knew that it was true.

"Then let me take you to your father," he said. "We shall make for you a carriage pulled by rays and bring you to the foot of the snowy mountains."

"No," said the Ice Queen. "I cannot now return to my father's house with my hair snapped and broken and the heart of the ocean in my eyes. I shall remain here on this island; and this tower, once my prison, shall become my home. I shall weave from the grass and the seaweed new tapestries, that the generations to come may not forget me."

Then the Mer-King delicately kissed the hand of the Ice Queen and dived back into the sea. The necklace of coral he lay in a pool on the rock. And the Queen picked it up and put it around her neck. It melted a small patch over her heart, for it was wet with the sea, but she never removed it. Every day for as long as she lived, she wove tapestries for the walls of her tower. And every night she would stand on the rocks and sing, and mariners would see from far off the mingling of the snowflakes with the spray, which was the love of the Ice Queen for the Mer-King.

The Man Without Desire

11

The Man Without Desire

The Man Without Desire is a little-known silent film from 1923, starring
Ivor Novello in the title role. The story is by director Adrian Brunel,
from an idea by Irish playwright Monckton Hoffe, and tells of a man
who sleeps for two hundred years and awakes without desire. In the
film, the same actors play eighteenth-century characters and their
twentieth-century descendants, creating a sense of mirroring.

It seems to draw on Robert Browning's poem 'A Toccata of
Galuppi's', which is quoted in the film:

> As for Venice and her people, *merely born to bloom and drop,*
> *Here on earth they bore their fruitage, mirth and folly were the crop:*
> *What of soul was left, I wonder, when the kissing had to stop?*

The story has the feel of a literary fairy tale. It is in part a gender-
reversed 'Sleeping Beauty' and uses many of the motifs found in
'The Glass Coffin' and 'The Half-Marble Prince'. From an asexual
perspective, it is problematic but deeply fascinating. This retelling is
by kind permission of Moving Image Library.

W as there ever a city that conjured up the Spirit of Romance
like Venice? Venice, where Doges wed the sea with rings.
Venice, where beauty wore a mask and the dagger lurked
beneath the cloak. Venice, where fortunes were staked in the Ridotto,
courtesans were richer than queens, and castrati made women swoon.

And was there ever a setting so contrary to the Venetian Spirit of
Romance than an English gentleman's study with its brown furniture,
its scent of leather and cigars? Yet here sat Professor Robert Mawdesley

and his three companions, awaiting the stroke of midnight.

"Gentlemen, you may wonder why I have summoned you at this hour," Mawdesley said. "The fact is, I have received instruction about a sum of money left me by a distant ancestor, and a letter to be opened at this precise date and time in the presence of a reputable lawyer, a physician learned in the arts of both East and West, and a representative of the bank."

With that, the hour struck, and the seal was broken. Mawdesley drew out a large sheaf of papers dated from the year seventeen-hundred and thirty-six.

"This looks to be a lengthy story," he observed. "But as it has not been told for almost two hundred years, we ought to give it our full attention."

The three settled in their armchairs as Mawdesley began to read:

There was in Venice, in the year seventeen-thirty-three, a young count named Vittorio Dandolo. He had fallen deeply in love with the beautiful Countess Leonora Almoro. Every night, like the troubadours of old, he would serenade her beneath her window. But Countess Leonora was a chaste wife, who would never dream of betraying her husband. Vittorio begged Leonora to let him be a friend to her, nothing more. He worshipped her but would do nothing to harm her honour.

Not so the Count. Like the libertine he was, Count Almoro was conducting an affair with a celebrated beauty known as La Foscolina. Nor was his dalliance a secret, for all his pretences at clandestine meetings. Indeed, it was the gossip of Venice, reported in a thinly veiled fashion by the *Venice Gazette*. The editor had it all from a maid in Almoro's household, who was the editor's lover.

When Almoro saw the newspaper report, he was incensed. He had men seize the editor and subject him to the cruellest punishment. The fingers that had dared write about the Count were to be crushed. Seeing them maimed and useless, said Almoro, would be a worse fate than losing them. The editor staggered from Almoro's dungeon in the arms of his sweetheart, vowing revenge.

Leonora begged her husband to end the affair, for the sake of their child, if nothing else. But this only outraged Almoro further.

"How dare you lecture me? I am lord and master in this house!" he bellowed and flung Leonora to the floor.

Leonora could not help but compare such behaviour with that of the gentle Vittorio. Desire was kindled in her heart. And though nothing but kisses passed between them, each longed for a way out of this dreadful situation.

It so happened that, living in Venice at that time was an Englishman named Simon Mawdesley, a scientist. One night, he was set upon by thieves outside his door. Vittorio was walking home from the Ridotto at that hour, and hearing the cries for help, hurried to the rescue. He chased the thieves away with drawn sword and carried the swooning Mawdesley into his shop.

What bizarre sights met Vittorio's eyes! Strange liquids bubbled in flasks, giving off pungent scents. Skeletons, skulls and the skins of strange beasts crowded on shelves or hung from the walls. Vittorio had never seen a room like it. Seating Mawdesley in a chair, he searched around for a drink to revive the man. He drew aside a curtain and was met by a truly horrifying sight. There was an open coffin with a man lying inside it!

"What was that?" he stammered, when he finally got a drink to Mawdesley's lips. "Behind the curtain. I saw..."

But the scientist was too shaken to reply.

"Another time." He waved his hand. "You will come again?"

"Of course," Vittorio promised.

When next he saw his new friend, Vittorio was shocked to see the man who had lain in the coffin walking about and helping Mawdesley to mix his potions.

"But I saw him," he said. "He was...in there."

"Yes, he was there for six weeks." Mawdesley smiled. "Suspended animation is my latest experiment."

"But how can that be possible?"

"Why should it not?" Mawdesley said. "There are accounts of Yogic trances going on for days or even weeks. Bodies have been found preserved in bogs, fish preserved in ice. Open your mind, Vittorio! So much is possible to the man of science."

But Vittorio had other matters with which to occupy his mind. Leonora was desperately unhappy, but how could she ever leave her child?

"Don't lose hope, my love," Vittorio wrote to her. "I will find a way to free you, I promise."

He sealed the note with a kiss and went to Palazzo Almoro, hoping Leonora's maid would give her the note. But when he arrived, another man was with the girl. It was the newspaper editor, come to take his revenge on Count Almoro. He gave a vial of poison to the maid, instructing her to slip it into Almoro's wine. Vittorio trembled at the news of the plot. Could this be his hoped-for chance? He handed the maid his note and she went inside the Palazzo, leaving Vittorio and the editor to wait in suspense.

Count Almoro was in a foul mood. La Foscolina had been nagging at him to prove his love to her, and all his wife did was sob and weep at him. He toyed with the decanter the maid had brought, watching the light glint from its glass stopper. The scent bottles on his toilette table glinted back, reflected in the expensive mirror.

His eyes narrowed. He could see a reflection in the mirror. The maid was watching him, peering through the curtains as though she expected something to happen. In three strides he crossed the room and seized her by the elbow.

"Why are you spying on me? This is some plot, isn't it? Tell me what's going on or by God..."

A note fell out of the girl's bosom. Almoro snatched it up and read.

"Vittorio Dandolo...and my wife...? Leonora! Come in here now! What is the meaning of this?" He thrust the paper in his wife's face. "You plan to betray me. With that fop, Dandolo. How long have you been his concubine?"

"I would never... Almoro, please. Think of our child," Leonora begged.

"And why is your maid spying on me? This wine is drugged, isn't it?"

"I don't know anything about it." Leonora was shaking.

"In that case, you drink it," said Almoro. "Then we'll know the truth."

Leonora's maid ran to the courtyard where Vittorio and the editor were waiting.

"Quick! Quick! My mistress is about to drink the poison."

Vittorio ran as if the hounds of hell were behind him, but it was too late. As he burst into the chamber, Leonora breathed her last and collapsed into his arms. He carried her to the couch and laid her upon it, as gently as if she had been sleeping. Then he turned to Almoro, who was standing, numbed, by the empty wine glass.

"Murderer!" Vittorio screamed.

He no longer knew what he was doing. All he knew was that Leonora was dead and Almoro was to blame. Before anyone could stop them, the two men had their hands around each other's throats. Vittorio's rage consumed him. His hands were a vice that wouldn't let go. Almoro convulsed one last time. His pulse ceased. He fell dead upon the floor.

Vittorio staggered back, horrified by the scene. He fell to his knees by Leonora's couch, kissing her beautiful, dead face. The maid grasped him by the shoulder.

"You must flee, my lord, before they find you here."

Unthinking, Vittorio ran. His legs carried him to Simon Mawdesley's house before he even knew where he was. Mawdesley pulled him inside and locked the door.

"You must help me." Vittorio collapsed into a chair and began to weep.

"My dear friend, whatever is the matter? Here, drink this." Mawdesley fussed around like an old nurse.

Vittorio gave a groan.

"Leonora is dead."

He poured out the whole tale into Mawdesley's ear.

"You must give me something to kill this pain. Surely, among all your potions and experiments..." Vittorio gazed around the bubbling flasks and vials.

Mawdesley plucked at his lip.

"There is something we can do, and I think you know what it is. You can take part in my greatest experiment by undergoing suspended animation. By the time you wake, this trouble will have blown over and you can begin again. But I have never put anyone under for such a length of time. I cannot guarantee it will work."

Vittorio glanced around as if he already heard the Watch pounding on the door.

"I'll try it," he said. "But in case it doesn't work, give me something that will end my misery for good."

They exchanged solemn glances.

"Very well," said Mawdesley, at last. He fetched a small vial and put it in Vittorio's pocket. "Only to be used in extreme need," he said.

He led Vittorio to the coffin. The sight of it filled Vittorio with horror, but he was too weary to contemplate another alternative. He lay down in the narrow casket.

"I must warn you, friend, that if this works and you awaken after your long sleep, it is likely you will not be the man you were. Your body will live but your soul will pay the price. Life may seem empty, bland, colourless. It is even possible you may find yourself without desire of any kind."

"I care not." Vittorio closed his eyes. "What use is desire without Leonora?"

Mawdesley nodded. He held out his arms and began the mesmeric gestures that would bring on the charmed sleep.

In the gentleman's study, Robert Mawdesley's guests shifted in their leather chairs.

"You don't mean to say this Dandolo chap is still alive? It's been nearly two hundred years."

The doctor rubbed his chin.

"Theoretically, it is possible, if the body is still intact. And you have the money for the enterprise. I say we go to Venice."

They arrived in a city that had seen better days, but whose canals and crumbling palazzos still spoke of former glories. With the help of the old letter and some locals, Professor Mawdesley and his doctor friend found the site of his ancestor's old shop. The secret chamber had been walled up, but workmen soon tore down the wall. Mawdesley and the doctor clambered over piles of old bricks into a darkened room, whose only feature was a coffin on a raised platform.

"This is it, then," said Mawdesley, with a shiver.

Together, they heaved the heavy wooden lid. Beneath it was a second lid, made of glass. Through it, they could see a face in repose. A man's face, delicate and attractive, framed by a powdered wig.

"Good God, it's him!" Mawdesley said.

They removed the second lid, and the doctor consulted the sheaf of old papers. Carefully, he incanted the words and made the gestures, as faithfully as possible to the written text. Then he stood back.

"I expect it will be some time before he fully awakes. I say we withdraw for a while, go to that little cafe across the street for a drink. The sight of modern people at the moment he opens his eyes could be too much of a shock for him."

Vittorio was left to awaken on his own. At first, he couldn't think where he was. His head was groggy, his legs were weak. He stumbled from the coffin, leaning on the wall for support. He had come...yes, he had come to Mawdesley's house. But where was Mawdesley? He peered across the rubble and brick dust. The shop was deserted. Vittorio rubbed his face, trying to think. Leonora! Had that all been a horrible dream, or had she really died in his arms? He must know. Staggering from the shop, he hurried to Palazzo Almoro.

It was still inhabited by the family, although their fortune had dwindled since Vittorio's day. The door was unlocked, and Vittorio raced upstairs to the salon. He glanced around him. The room looked... different. Ugly little tables cluttered up the floor space. The stucco was cracked and peeling.

A curtain parted and a woman came into the room. Vittorio's heart leapt to his throat.

"Leonora!"

He rushed to take her in his arms. She was not dead, after all. It had all been a hideous dream, and now they would never be parted.

"What are you doing? Get off me! Who are you?"

The woman pushed him away, furious. Vittorio stared at her. She had Leonora's face, but Leonora would never have worn her hair so short and frizzy about her neck, or her dress so scandalously revealing.

"You're not Countess Leonora Almoro?" he said. "Where is she?"

"What do you mean, where is she?" The woman looked at Vittorio as if he was insane. "She was my ancestor. She's in the family crypt, of course."

At that moment, Mawdesley and the doctor came bursting in.

"So sorry about our friend, miss. We should have known he'd come here. He's...not been well."

And with that, they took Vittorio away, to begin his new life in nineteen-twenty-three.

There were many things Vittorio found astonishing about his new world: matches, motor boats, telephones. Yet so much of it seemed drab by comparison to the life he knew. In his new apartment, Mawdesley and the doctor persuaded Vittorio to abandon his silk stockings and knee breeches, his velvet coat with silver stitching, in favour of a herringbone suit and Oxford brogues. His hair was cut short and slicked back with brilliantine. What a sorry figure he cut, compared to the man he had once been! Instead of a sword, he must carry a walking cane. Instead of a tricorn, tabarro cloak and mask, a humble Fedora sat on his head. And where was he to go? The Ridotto was long since gone, and the gondolas were filled with tourists. Little wonder, then, that he was drawn back to the Palazzo Almoro, and to Genevra, who so resembled his lost Leonora.

Genevra (for that was the young woman's name) had received a telephone call from Mawdesley to explain about "the man in fancy dress". She didn't pretend to understand it all, but she found Vittorio interesting. He was always impeccably polite, kissing her hand and that of her mother. The old people were charmed by his old-fashioned manners and declared him a much finer match than Genevra's current suitor, her cousin Count Gardi-Almoro.

What a moment that was, when the two men first met! By some trick of heredity, Gardi-Almoro resembled almost exactly the hated Count Almoro of yesteryear. Vittorio trembled with horror and repulsion. Gardi-Almoro was likewise repulsed. Just who was this odd stranger who was stealing Genevra's affections? True, Genevra was a little insipid for the Count's taste, and it wasn't as if he had no other women to warm his bed, but he had his reputation and status to think of. Surely the Almoros would not allow this Vittorio Dandolo to steal away the match he deserved?

And what did Vittorio think? Genevra interested him, yet she was not Leonora. He was unsure what to make of the modern girl who showed herself so shamelessly to the world, talking on the telephone and rouging her lips in public. Where was the subtle language of the fan, the chaste glance from a balcony? The Grand Romance of Old Venice was gone, and with it...yes, Vittorio's desire. He remembered now the words of the scientist Simon Mawdesley: *Your body will live but your soul will pay the price. Life may seem empty, bland, colourless. It is even possible you may find yourself without desire of any kind.*

But he couldn't allow Genevra to wed Gardi-Almoro and so let history repeat itself. This time, Vittorio would be her husband and protector. The necessary desire would come to him once he was married. Perhaps...

It was not to be. His new wife expected much more than friendship, but Vittorio had nothing more to give. In time, both grew frustrated.

Vittorio thought more and more of the old days, poring over old prints by Canaletto and toying with the swords that hung on the Palazzo wall. Genevra began secretly corresponding with Gardi-Almoro. The man might be a cad but at least he knew how to excite a girl. They arranged a rendezvous in the gardens, one evening when Gardi-Almoro was taking supper at the Palazzo. At an arranged time, Gardi-Almoro tipped Genevra the wink and slipped out into the night.

When Vittorio realised what was happening, he burned with anger and shame. He chased after Gardi-Almoro to confront him.

"You're nothing but a common seducer." He spat out the words. Memories of a previous century loomed in his mind. An empty wine glass. Leonora struggling for her last breath. "You will not escape me this time *Count Almoro!*"

With that he hurled himself at his rival, reaching for a stranglehold.

"Stop! Stop it both of you, this instant!"

Genevra ran into the garden, her dress flapping. She seized both men by the arms. With a sigh, Vittorio felt the fight go out of him. He dragged his feet back indoors and sank into a chair. Genevra followed him.

"So...you are in love with him now?" Vittorio didn't even look up.

"Actually, no, I don't love him." Genevra's voice began to rise. "But I'd rather be with him than in this cold mockery of a marriage. I have been cheated, do you hear me? Cheated!"

"Please, Genevra." Vittorio took her hand. "Let me try again to make you happy."

"*You* make me happy! You – a man without a heart!" Genevra gave a bitter laugh.

Slowly, Vittorio got up and made his way to his study. The walls, the furniture, everything seemed bleached of colour. He sat at his desk and took out pen and paper.

My dear Genevra,

My life and love are of the past. It was selfish of me to wed you. You deserve so much more than I can give. I am going away now. You will be free. Forgive me.

Vittorio

He gave the note to a maid, asking her not to give it to her mistress until morning. Then he dragged out a trunk from under a table and opened it up. Inside it were all his eighteenth-century effects. There was his coat with the silver stitching, and there in the pocket was the vial given him by Simon Mawdesley: *Only to be used in extreme need.*

Vittorio unstopped the vial and drank the contents in one draught. He looked about the room. No, he would not die like this. He pulled his old clothes from the trunk and began unbuttoning his jacket.

In the meantime, Genevra's maid had become worried.

"The master gave me this. He didn't seem himself," she said.

As soon as Genevra had read the note, she hurried to her husband's room as fast as she could. Vittorio was sitting in an antique chair, dressed in his old velvet suit and lace-trimmed chemise. His face was salt-white; his chest heaved for breath. Tears pricked Genevra's eyes. She knelt at Vittorio's side and took his hands.

"Vittorio, don't leave me. I was wrong. We can start again."

She took his head in her hands and began to kiss him. And in that moment, Vittorio was back in the Venice of old, serenaded under the stars as gondolas drifted by. He buried his fingers in Genevra's hair and kissed her with tender passion. Then, the hour struck. Count Vittorio Dandolo, the man without desire, breathed his last.

The Lost Children
of Lorenwald

12

The Lost Children of Lorenwald

In Greek myth, the nymph Daphne turns into a tree in order to escape the amorous pursuit of the god Apollo. 'The Lost Children of Lorenwald' plays with that idea, combining it with motifs from 'The Pied Piper of Hamelin' and the group of fairy tales known as 'The Singing Bones', in which a victim's remains cry out for justice. By contrast with some traditional fairy tales, I wanted to create a wholly positive portrayal of asexuality, one that would be reassuring to the asexual community and to family and friends. The central figure of the Storysinger emphasises the importance of speaking out, of telling our story, in order that others might not feel alone.

'The Lost Children of Lorenwald' first appeared in *The Forgotten & the Fantastical 3* (2017).

Every forest tells a story.

Broadleaf or pine. Sunny or tangled. Autumn or spring. Each forest has its own unique song to sing, its own tale to tell. And it is the craft of the Storysinger to gather those tales and sing them to whoever will listen.

It was neither autumn nor spring when I came to Lorenwald, but the lazy end of summer, when fruits hang heavy on the raspberry canes and the sunset sky is abuzz with tiny wings. I was too early for the cider harvest, but I drank my small beer in the common room of the tumbledown inn and nodded my thanks for the plate of cheese and black bread.

"What brings you to these parts, aunty?"

The hostess wiped her hands on her apron and watched me eat with scrutiny, no doubt waiting for my reaction to her home baking.

I smiled. In this part of the country, every woman of my age was "aunty". Once, I had been hailed as "daughter", but those days were far behind me; a few more years and I would be "gammer".

"I go into the forest to collect songs," I said. "I'll give you a tale or two from other parts after supper." I patted the hurdy-gurdy that lay on the bench beside me. "I expect you don't get news very often in this neighbourhood."

In most local taverns, this offer was usually met with a roar of approval, along with requests for popular ballads and love songs. Here, the only sound was the thud of a tankard on the table, as every pair of eyes in the room fixed a cold stare in my direction. Even the wasps seemed to stop buzzing.

"No one goes into the Lorenwald," said the host, his voice like granite. "By Order of the Village Council. It is a cursed place."

"Forgive me, I don't mean to cause offence." I took care to smile as I spoke. "But I have walked many, many woods in my time. I know their ways as well as you know the art of brewing. Most supposed curses and hauntings are simply a misunderstanding of nature's ways. I have never encountered anything more dangerous than a boar or wolf. And I am well equipped to deal with those." I showed the horn and knife at my belt.

The host's expression never changed.

"No one goes into the Lorenwald," he said. "We lost our children there."

Children get lost in the woods. It happens. In their innocence, they stray from the path, only to fall foul of the elements, wild beasts or – God forbid – unscrupulous humans. When it happens, it is a tragedy that can tear out the heart of a community. I knew that well enough not to press the host and hostess any further that night.

But to avoid the forest because of that tragedy was to seal off part of the heart and to refuse to let it grow again. I could not leave the village without at least trying to set it on the road to healing. So, I told the hostess I would stay a few nights and I offered simple songs for my keep: harvest carols that fitted with the season, full of fruitfulness and plenty. Tales of sorrow would keep for now.

In the morning, I went to the churchyard. I wandered among the graves in the golden glow of dawn. There were child graves, as there always are. Such is the way of life. But there was nothing that spoke of unquiet rest or the kind of communal trauma I had sensed in the common room.

When the sun became hot, I retreated to the cool and shade of the church. In most ways, it was like other country churches in these parts: whitewashed walls, a covered pulpit, simple pews. But between two of the windows was a memorial plaque in bas-relief, the like of which I had never seen in any church. It depicted youths and maidens dancing as they might do on a May morning, their heads crowned with flowers. On one side they were smiling, showing coy pleasure in each other's charms. But on the other side, their expressions became glassy. Trees plucked at their clothes and overshadowed their heads with branches. At the extreme edge of the picture, the young people could no longer be seen. A tangle of trees hid them from sight.

Beneath the image was a simple inscription:

To the children of Lorbeerwald, now called Lorenwald.
The forest took them.

Over the next few days, I questioned people as subtly as I could. A chat with old wives as we washed our clothes together at the village well. A tale of old times with the blacksmith's aged father, in exchange for news of distant lands. Some were as stony as the tavern host, refusing to speak if I so much as mentioned the forest. With others, a torrent of words gushed forth, as if their mouths had been dammed for years. A beloved daughter. A treasured son. When the young people had taken to the woods on May Day, as young folk did, their child had left the group alone, never to return. It was thirty years ago. Six-and-thirty. Twenty-five. One woman whispered in my ear that her daughter had been the last, nineteen summers ago. That was the year the Village Council had declared the forest a forbidden place. A man not yet thirty showed me the brand on his left hand that he had received for snaring rabbits. He had only been trying to feed his family, he told me. His daughter could be out picking berries in the Lorenwald now, were it not for the Council's ban.

That evening at dusk, I crept as close to the eaves of the Lorenwald as I could without being seen. Unlike the depiction on the church plaque, the trees were smooth-barked and graceful, with wide clearings in-between. The last of the day's sunshine cast golden pools of light on the forest floor.

The perfect spot for dancing – and for other pleasures that might follow. I smiled; my own youth seemed very distant now, but I had not forgotten.

Perhaps the young people had simply run away together? A secret tryst in the woods, perhaps with youngsters from a neighbouring village, and then away to a new life? This did not seem the kind of forest where a youngster could lose their way, especially a local lass or lad familiar with its paths.

I crept closer. Already, I could sense the edges of a song, reaching out towards me. There was peace in its voice, stillness, serenity. I frowned, struggling to catch it. Another level was hidden behind the first, older, deeper. A struggle? Fear? Flight? If only I knew more!

A twig cracked behind me.

"Curfew has already tolled, aunty. It's time you were asleep in bed."

The host's face was a stony mask. I nodded my head and followed him back to the inn.

I had to get into the wood.

A forest's song can only be heard when you stand under its canopy; its earth under your feet, its scent in your nostrils. I waited until the sky had turned to the mauves and sapphires of a summer's night, and the villagers were all abed. They were country folk, working hard and rising early, hoping to make the most of the morning's light. They would sleep soundly.

I took a dark-lantern, checked the knife and horn at my belt, and made my way along the overgrown path to the Lorenwald. A few milky stars showed in the deep blue overhead. It was an enchanted night, a night made for young lovers.

The song I had heard on the eaves of the wood grew stronger as I walked beneath its shade. Peace. Fulfilment. Freedom. This was not a story that had ended in tragedy, whatever the church plaque said. But there was something else that had come before. Something the youngsters had come to the wood to escape. They had begged the trees to take them in. Had I heard that aright? Gently, I put my hand on the green-grey trunk of an ash tree. The energy beneath my palm was palpable.

Tell them. Was I imagining these words? *Make them understand. Our choice. Our lives.* I had never felt energy so powerful. Was the spirit of the lost children somehow within these trees? I moved my hand to a neighbouring trunk. The song was the same.

Tell them we miss them. Make them understand, Storysinger. The cry was becoming more urgent. Make them understand what? That the children of the Lorenwald had gone...where? *Tell them, this is who we are.* There was a vibration in the ground, a rustle of foliage in the distance. Someone was coming. *Tell them, Storysinger.* I had minutes left. I took out my knife and cut a dry branch from the base of the trunk.

Not a moment too soon. Lights were bobbing through the forest. A few breaths later, and I could see the faces of the host and several greybeards, stern-faced beneath their hoods.

"You will come with us, Storysinger," the host said. "You will pay the price for breaking our law."

The branch in my hand wailed.

A court had been set up in the inn-yard. The host and six others – the Village Council, I presumed – sat at a long bench at one end. The other villagers sat at tables with ale mugs or watched from the stables. Playing children were shushed and scolded. This was a serious matter, and most of the faces showed it.

I could hear my own heartbeat as I rose to give my defence. The penalty for entering the wood was branding. Not only would I be unable to play an instrument for months, but the brand on my palm would mark me out as a criminal wherever I went. I would lose the only livelihood I had.

I toyed with the dry branch in my hand. All night, I had been whittling away at it, as much to keep away fears as for any notion of how I might use it. It now had the form of a rustic flute, hollow inside with holes for mouth and fingers. A speaking flute. I had heard of such things in tales. But could a makeshift flute speak in such a way that any but a Storysinger could hear it?

I licked my dry lips.

"My good host, members of the Council, good people of Lorenwald." As a Storysinger, I had been trained to make my voice carry, and now every head lifted. "I will not make excuses for myself. I know I broke your rules. I simply ask that you pay attention to the voices of your own children, who left this village for the sanctuary of the Lorenwald. They were not stolen from you, as you suppose. Neither are they far from you now. Hear their song."

I put the flute to my lips and breathed life into the dry wood. I barely knew what I expected to hear, but the voice that came forth was one I will never forget. Sorrowful and serene, gentle and pure, it was the voice of the forest itself:

Forgive us, dear parents, if you cannot understand. We grew up among you, but you never truly saw us. While our companions longed to unite with each other as one flesh, we wished only to preserve the intactness of our own bodies. When you spoke of your hopes and plans for our marriages, we feared the bridal chamber. When the Rites of May drew others to take our hands, to speak to us with words of desire, we were afraid. We begged the sheltering forest to let us in. Our prayers were answered. Before our pursuers could catch us, our bodies were ringed with bark, our fingers turned to foliage. We became free to live our lives intact, graceful and growing.

Do not reject us, dear parents. Do not forsake us, although we are changed. Walk among us once more. We will shelter you. In life and death, we will watch over you. We are your sons and daughters: Haldis, Gyda, Armand, Nordika, Elrod...

As the litany of names sang out, one after another of the villagers crossed themselves, fell to their knees, wept on each other's shoulders. When the song ended, I lowered my flute and was silent. I looked at the host. He sat with his head in his hands, sobbing like a baby.

I left Lorenwald a few days later. My pack on my back and my knife at my belt, I took the road down the valley, headed for the next village eager to welcome a Storysinger.

But not before I had witnessed a sight I will treasure all my days. Men and women, their hair grey with age, walking under the eaves of the Lorenwald. Some walked hand-in-hand as couples; others walked singly and alone. Most had tears in their eyes. I saw a light of recognition in their faces as each approached a particular tree. I saw them embrace the grey-green trunks, kiss their lost children, sit beneath their shady boughs. Before I left, many an aged parent had taken up the strains of an old lullaby or well-loved tale.

It will be many years before I visit Lorenwald again. When I do, the villagers will no doubt call me "gammer". The old folks I left beneath the trees may well lie buried under them. But I will not forget what happened here, when the lost children were found once more.

Story Sources and Further Reading

Arnold, Matthew. "The Forsaken Merman". 1849.

Asbjörnsen & Moe. *East of the Sun & West of the Moon: Old Tales from the North* trans. Sir GW Dasent. New York: George H Doran Company, 1920.

Browning, Robert. "A Toccata of Galuppi's". 1855.

Brunel, Adrian (dir.). *The Man Without Desire*. UK: Atlas Biocraft, 1923.

Burton, Sir Richard Francis. *A plain and literal translation of the Arabian nights entertainments, now entitled The book of a thousand nights and a night. Volume 1.* The Burton Club for private subscribers only, 1885.

Byatt, AS. *Possession: A Romance*. London: Chatto & Windus Ltd, 1990.

Caldecott, Moyra. *Crystal Legends*. Wellingborough: The Aquarian Press, 1990.

Cawley, AC & Anderson, JJ (ed.). *Sir Gawain & the Green Knight, Pearl, Cleanness, Patience*. London: Everyman, 1991.

Chrétien de Troyes. *Arthurian Romances*, trans. DDR Owen. London: Everyman, 1993.

Cox, Susan McNeill. *The Complete Tale of Troylus and Zellandine from the "Perceforest" Novel: An English Translation, from Merveilles & contes Vol. 4 No. 1* (May 1990). JSTOR: Wayne State University Press, 2015.

Grimm, J & W. *Household Stories*. London: George Routledge & Sons, 1853.

Irwin, Robert. *The Arabian Nights: A Companion*. London: I.B. Tauris, 2003.

James, Grace. *Green Willow & Other Japanese Fairy Tales*. London: Macmillan and Co Limited, 1910.

Lang, Andrew. *The Green Fairy Book*. 1892.

Lang, Andrew. *The Arabian Nights Entertainments*. 1898.

MacDonald, George. *Phantastes: A Faerie Romance*. 1858.

Malory, Sir Thomas. *Works*, ed. Eugène Vinaver. Oxford: OUP, 1971.

Marie de France. *The Lais of Marie de France*, trans. Glyn S Burgess & Keith Busby. London: Penguin, 1986.

Matthews, John. *The Arthurian Tradition*. Shaftesbury: Element, 1994.

Meade, Michael. "Truth and Forgetfulness". *The Living Myth Podcast* #85, www.livingmyth.org: 2018.

Ozaki, Yei Theodora. *The Japanese Fairy Book*. New York: EP Dutton & Co, 1903.

Ovid. *Metamorphoses*, trans. David Raeburn. London: Penguin, 2004.

Plato. *Symposium*, trans. Benjamin Jowett. The Internet Classics Archive, classics.mit.edu: 1994-2009.

Rose, Graham & King, Peter. *The Love of Roses*. London: Quiller Press, 1990.

Schönwerth, Franz Xaver von. *The Turnip Princess and Other Newly Discovered Fairy Tales*, ed. Erika Eichenseer, trans. Maria Tatar. New York: Penguin, 2015.

Starling, Amelia. "Sleeping Beauty and the Fates of Mythology". *Centre for Myth Studies at the University of Essex*, essexmyth.wordpress.com: 29th May 2017.

Starling, Amelia. "Sleeping Beauty: The Meaning of Fate, Sleep and Death". *The Willow Web*, thewillowweb.com: 2017.

Takahata, Isao (dir.). *The Tale of the Princess Kaguya*. Japan: Studio Ghibli, 2013.

Tatar, Maria (ed.). *The Cambridge Companion to Fairy Tales*. Cambridge: CUP, 2015.

Tennyson, Lord Alfred. "The Lady of Shalott". 1833.

Tresidder, Megan. *The Language of Love: A Celebration of Love and Passion*. London: Duncan Baird, 2004.

Zipes, Jack (ed.). *The Original Folk & Fairy Tales of the Brothers Grimm: The Complete First Edition*. Princeton: PUP, 2014.

Acknowledgements

A huge thanks to family and friends who have supported and encouraged me through the long process of coming out and sharing my story (and my stories) with the world. You helped me to be brave.

Many thanks to AVEN (The Asexual Visibility & Education Network) for believing in this project and helping me get it off the ground. And to all those who have championed it on social media, even though we have never met. Thank you to Helen Hart at SilverWood Books for agreeing to publish this book. And of course, to our Kickstarter supporters. We could not have done it without you!

Thanks as always to Swanwick Writers' Summer School. Without the support and inspiration of my fellow "Swanwickers" I wouldn't be where I am today. Thanks to the Brick Box Rooms in Bradford for giving me a safe place to express myself.

And finally, thanks to everyone who played their part in introducing me to fairy tales, myths and legends. From my grandparents to my English teachers to my tutors at the University of Leeds School of English. I thank you from the bottom of my heart.

Supporters

This book has been crowdfunded by Kickstarter. Many thanks to our generous supporters listed and to those who remain anonymous.

Matis
Peggy Brett
Dannie K
Kristen Gee
Caitlin M
James Peebles Brown
Jennifer Beltrame
Holly
Anna
Kae Em
Rachael Perkins
Haviland Forrister
Clara McCoy
Chrysilla Fisher
Al Gad
Zoe Jones
Victoria Silber
Ginevra
Raven Ford
Wren Godwin
Hazor
Cuddly Tiger
SMason

Diane Smith
neverwhere
Jordan Schneider
Katrina Allis
Dehlinger
Kathryn Henriques
Brad Roberts
Micah
Alice Foster
Christy Pratt
Sara
Mairi White
Amy (Other Amy)
Donna
Dimitra Stathopoulos
SuperDustin83
Alexis Paperman
Stacey M
Wil Bastion
em-j hill
The Selkie Delegation
Jojo Stewart
Julie Dick

Natasha Chisdes
Mark Sabellico
Mikayla Hutchinson
Kathleen Murray
Sarah
Lily Finley
Dagmar
Rylin
Dr Teika Bellamy
Katie Fane
Narrelle M Harris
Kyle Johnson
smwl16
Rhianna Drinkwater
Amy
Brydon Caldwell
Amaryllis Quilliou
Amelia
Anna Toretha Keegan
Megan Krantz
Thomas Barsby
Anya Scoble-Hansen
Paul Hiscock

Austin Howard
Kayla
Anita gray Saito
Rachel Smith
Abbie Faulkner
John Walters
Raven
Karen
Kathleen Doerr
Santos Torres
Lauren Wallace
JC
Ruthan
Keely Lawrence
Adrienne
Edward Benjamin
Hunter
Christine
Mariah Griffin
S Jordan
Kailey
Laura Norman
Sophia Lidestri
Paige Liberski
Kit S.
Kevin Brazel
haley
Cecelia Barrett
Thomas
Scott Mackie
Alexandru Nedel
Mackenzie Woolf
Randissimo
Colin-Roy Hunter
Candace Ashley
C
Monty Nero

Claire Lower
Hannah
Nicole Madden
Clinton Davis
Constance
Zoe
Sophy Brough
Emma Browning
Denise
Laura C
Neil Graham
Christine Marson
Veronica Ball
Joanne McCuaig
Allison Sunderhaus
David Seppi
Esmeralda "Ezzy"
    Guerrero-Languzzi
Permafry_42
Maria Tschakert
Quinn Pollock
Jess Draws
Stig Conradi
Rønningen
Andrea Brin
Ariel Button
Andrew John
Thomas Bull
Pate McKissack
Lya
Melissa
Lauren Kahre
Ergane
Stephanie Afonso
Jeannette Ng
Sharnell Clair
Carolyn

neotoma
Kerenza
Lynn
Amalia Boris
Narwhal design
Aster
Joey Pedras
Doug Edwards
Stephanie Feliciano
Brittany Wilbert
Maggie
Tessa Eaton
Vida Cruz
Beppo
Emilie
Delclaux-Hammon
Alyson
Hannah Ackermans
Laura Fitzgerald
Georgina Toland
Anke Wehner
Lauren C Hamell
Katarzyna Karczewska
Zachariah Candelaria
Icewine Rose
Jess Schlimmer
Sia
Kay Black
twonkykitty
Abigail Scott
Kaiqua
Eruvadhril
Micaela Godfrey
JennyS
Molly Lohman
Heath
Quinn Weller

filkferengi
Casey
Kirsty Morgan
Christine
Hilary McNeill
Ben Fletcher
Kristīne Vītola
August
Satya Sinha
Arcnes
Natasha Liff
PAul trinies
Drew Jackson
Suzanne Hillman
susanreads
Minerva Cerridwen
Ambrose Zen
Sen Keen
Steve Savitzky
Lauraluce
Solomon Michaels
Tasha Turner
Sean C Davis
Katherine Hempel
Claire Rosser
Rachel
Amy Swahlan
Edith Olenius
Kat
Laura
Andrea Speed
Tifa Robles
kardia1122
Marie
Jessica
Mallory
Charly Olson

Guest 233683787
GamerGeekJordan
T Helm
Criss Forshay
William Pettibone
Misti Coronel
Rebecca Politzer
Guest 1925931001
Mirva Lukkari
Wendy Grace Mehner
Lilja Kupua Bayley
Christiy Webb
Kathryn Slater
Komal
Lali
Raymond
Deborah Hawkins
Alex Villanueva
Satsu
Molly Lankford Roth
das-t
Guest 1404178809
David Noller
Guest 347921439
Kari Blocker
Ivan Andrus
Amanda Stone
Lauren McCormick
Guest 994728469
Guest 316109086
Emma Broderick
Jennifer Danyluk
Austin Atherton
Emily Metcalfe
Ying Tang
Kari Holman
Lisa

Robyn Bennis
James Marsters
Kerry Green
Leah Robin
Joelle Renstrom
Ben Perkins
Elaine Isaak
Evergreen Lee
Anna Pittenger
Stephanie Keahey
Niki Turner
Jaymie Horak
Dev Singer
Charis Papavassilis
Cheryl Holland
Valerie Pfister
Audrey
Danielle McAuley
Nina Brottman
Michael and Liz
CRR
Haviva Avirom
James Smith
Antti Hallamäki
Guest 29751053
Ash Jenkins
Guest 1177880419
Christina Potter
William
Anett Šubrtová
Lila Duga
Kenn Martin
Andrea Gonzalez
Emily Hogarth
K Hunt
Shayna Sessler
Insa Miller

Maddy
Meghan O'Sullivan
Ellen Howse
Nightsky
JD Martell
Erin Webb
Cedar Skye Kilcrease
Guest 1471239395
AURELIA LEO
Jennifer Boyer
Matthew Searle
Lauren Joy Moor
Guest 545088986
Guest 1727941148
PyrrhaIphis
Ellen
Heidi Biersborn
Maggie
Jessica Oehrlein
Serpent_moon
Orianna Keating
Veronika
Tamar Godel
Megara Sanderson
Amy
Lindsey Petrucci
Guest 1424489271
Lorena Carrington
metalgabu
Sophia
Bisignano-Vadino
Guest 1509791660
Kreeblah
Ingrid Jendrzejewski
Alexandra
Jen O'C
Jess Turner

Sarah
Lizzy Scheers
Ezra Lee
Nicole
Jaylee James
Chloe Arnall
mojosam
Lisa Hunt
Kerri Regan
Ann Penn
Lauren Kell
Jasmine Wolf
Dubious Merit
Guest 2001217831
Guest 1767982802
Ernie Prang
AJ HAYDON
Guest 1702249187
Natasha Ali
Chris Piazzo
Joe Theaker
Sarah MacQueen
David Goodsell
Rosie Prince
Mick Quirk
M Ryder
Olivia Montoya
Valerie Kaplan
Alycia Shedd
Elizabeth Evans-Gist
Sam Karpierz
Andy Yeoh
Guest 69114750
Margaret Clark
Tawny Rose Case
Guest 1698229545
The Creative Fund

Helen Lobel
Melanie Nazelrod
IcyOshawottz

www.ingramcontent.com/pod-product-compliance
Lightning Source LLC
Chambersburg PA
CBHW031240260626
47169CB00007B/2388